LITHUANIA

JOHNS HOPKINS: POETRY AND FICTION
John T. Irwin, General Editor

FICTION TITLES IN THE SERIES

Guy Davenport, *Da Vinci's Bicycle: Ten Stories*

Stephen Dixon, *Fourteen Stories*

Jack Matthews, *Dubious Persuasions*

Guy Davenport, *Tatlin!*

Joe Ashby Porter, *The Kentucky Stories*

Stephen Dixon, *Time to Go*

Jack Matthews, *Crazy Women*

Jean McGarry, *Airs of Providence*

Jack Matthews, *Ghostly Populations*

Jean McGarry, *The Very Rich Hours*

Steve Barthelme, *And He Tells the Little Horse the Whole Story*

Michael Martone, *Safety Patrol*

Jerry Klinkowitz, *"Short Season" and Other Stories*

James Boylan, *Remind Me to Murder You Later*

Frances Sherwood, *Everything You've Heard Is True*

Stephen Dixon, *All Gone: Eighteen Short Stories*

Jack Matthews, *Dirty Tricks*

Joe Ashby Porter, *Lithuania*

LITHUANIA

---

short stories by

Joe Ashby Porter

Joe Ashby Porter

Sewanee 8/92

for Charles, with admiration, fondly —

— Joe

THE JOHNS HOPKINS UNIVERSITY PRESS

Baltimore and London

This book has been brought to publication with the generous assistance of the G. Harry Pouder Fund.

Printed in the United States of America

The John Hopkins University Press
701 West 40th Street
Baltimore, Maryland 21211
The Johns Hopkins Press Ltd., London

The paper used in this book meets the minimum requirements of American National Standard for Information Sciences—Permanence of Paper for Printed Library Materials, ANSI Z39.48-1984.

Library of Congress Cataloging-in-Publication Data and permissions are on p. 147.

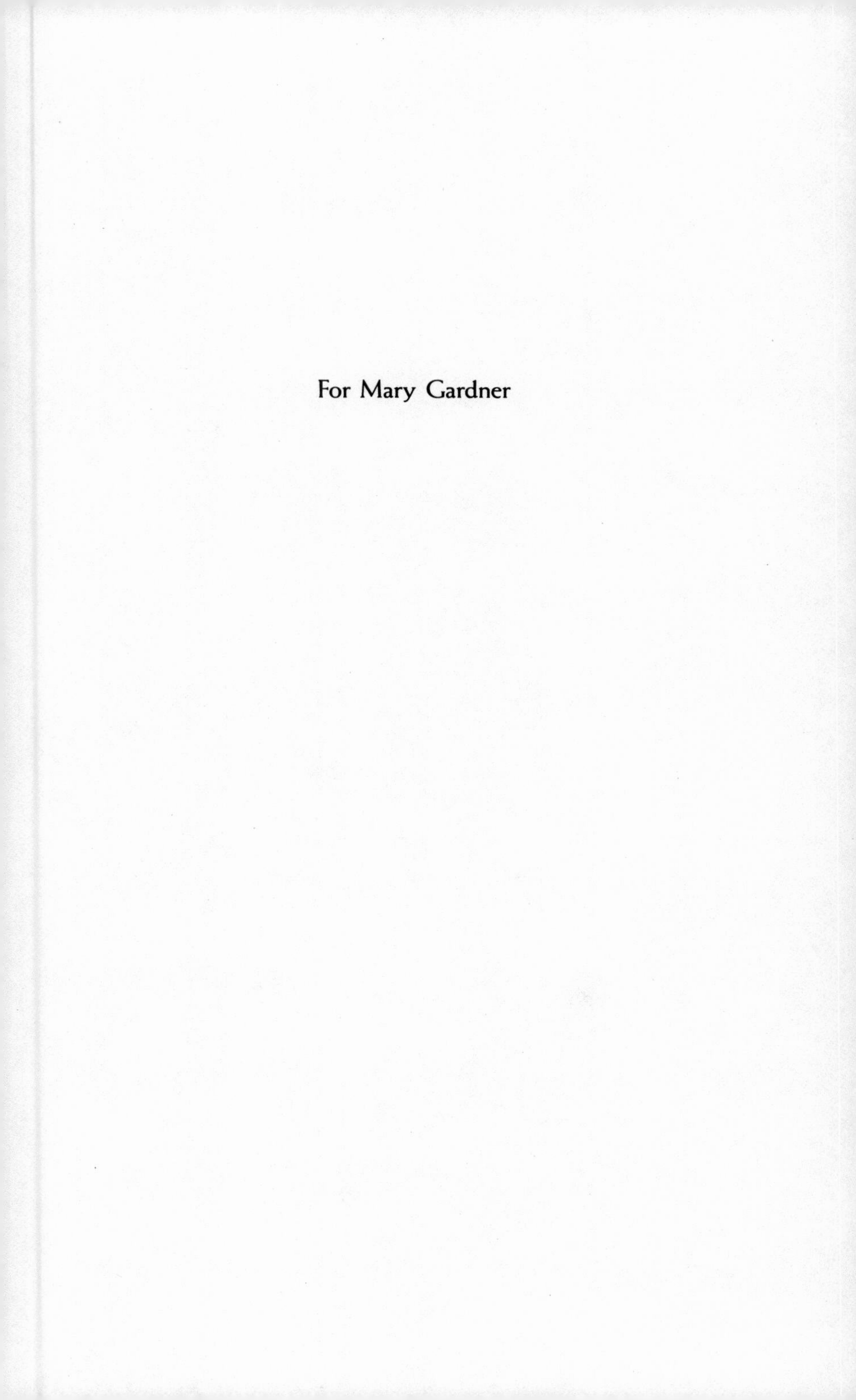

For Mary Gardner

A. It is a country and no country. With only the briefest official recognition years ago, it nevertheless persists in minds, and even maintains legations. Its stony name bears the trace of an element used to treat some manias.

Q. What is Lithuania?

Contents

CONTES

Conte n. m. (de *conter*). Court récit, en prose ou en vers, d'événements merveilleux ou tirés de la réalité. . . . Discours ou récit mensonger . . .

Nouveau Petit Larousse illustré, 1955

———Masculine noun (from *to recount*). Short account, in prose or verse, of marvels or events drawn from reality. . . . Untrue discourse or narrative . . .

Aerial View

Ten years ago (already! it hardly seems possible) my French friend Yves and I took the twenty-four-hour boat trip from Marseille to Tunis. It was April, and we would spend a month traveling in Tunisia. Yves and his parents are among the colonial French who left Tunisia in 1961 after the three-day war, and part of the purpose of the trip was for him to see his birthplace again. We were both in our early thirties, a little old for the sort of adventure we were embarked on; old, but there anyway. We boarded at ten in the morning and by noon were out of sight of Europe on a rocking sea much bigger than Ulysses' wine-dark one.

The romance and anxiety of the crossing had evaporated by nightfall. To save money for later, we tried to sleep sitting in the lounge with Arab laborers returning from stints in France and Germany who suffered terrible bouts of seasickness through the long night. I finally dozed a few hours before dawn and woke to near and distant snoring in the weak light.

Out on the deck I found Yves talking with a stocky middle-aged Arab who seemed to have suffered no ill effects from the ship's movement. Leaning against the rail, he wore a cream wool burnoose against the sea wind. I seemed to recall bleary glimpses of him through the night smoking cigarettes and keeping watch over the sleepers. He was smoking now, and his brown eyes turned toward me as Yves introduced us and I spoke my halting French. He was Taieb ben Khalifa, returning from a business trip to Paris, wholesaling Tunisian fig brandy. Under the lightening sky my sleeplessness made me hallucinate that he and Yves were talking about me in their rapid French as I stood with them. I thought about being shanghaied to Tanzania or Yemen. Years after, when stateside friends met, they might work out only that I'd disappeared abroad. And yet Taieb with his coppery powdery skin, his eyes that seemed too wise to move much, and too discreet—he'd almost have been a bearable slaver, I thought.

Slowly by slowly the boat proceeded through the wide Tunis harbor to its dock where it geared down into a shuddering reverse and at last had insensibly touched. The bustling passengers, recovered from the crossing, had washed and combed and perfumed themselves and now waved from the ship's railing, and one wife held up a cage for her goldfinch to see its new home. In the customs shed an official shepherded everyone through to waiting families and friends and taxis. Mr. Taieb explained that the city center was two kilometers west and suggested sharing a cab. Hunger had so routed sleepiness and timidity that as waterfront gave way to Moorish-modern city center I asked Mr. Taieb to suggest a place for lunch for Yves and me.

Half an hour later he had insisted on paying for the taxi and was leading us to a restaurant. A crowd, with few of the women veiled, obstructed one intersection. In the center, under a billowing two-story cloth poster of an angry Bourguiba, a uniformed policewoman was directing traffic. It was she, Mr. Taieb explained, who had drawn the crowd—before today, no Tunisian woman had ever directed traffic.

At l'Etoile de Nabeul on a narrow street where the new city gave way to the souk the three of us had a quiet table in a walled garden with two orange trees in bloom. Taieb recommended couscous, Yves seconded, and I concurred.

The waiter greeted Mr. Taieb by name and welcomed Yves and me to Tunisia. "You," he said with courtly blandness to a smiling Yves, "you I'm actually welcoming back, it seems." And so I settled into a long lunch during which my slow French kept me from saying much and so let me pay unusual attention—to the octopus salad and couscous, to the bird song and perfume from the orange tree behind me, to the restaurant's other patrons, all Arab males and most middle-aged, and to my companions.

Mr. Taieb had been born in the old Tunis medina and now lived a few kilometers away in the Cité Bouchoucha with his wife and youngest child, Aisha, who at fourteen was showing unsettling rebelliousness. His other daughter and three sons were married and raising families of their own, all in or near Tunis, except for Habib, who had gone away to Foum Tatahouine "to work for Bourguiba's electric company." Midway through the meal a jasmine vendor came in off the street. At the next table a younger man, after some joking with his friends, bought one of the buds and tucked it behind his ear.

After the meal Mr. Taieb by some sleight of hand paid the bill before Yves's and my very eyes. I was stammering thanks—heartfelt thanks, given my budget—when Mr. Taieb said, "No, it's nothing. When I come to U.S.A. you can do the same. Look: the U.N. is meeting here for lunch, all friendly. Tunisia is France's ex-colony, U.S.A. is everybody's papa now, but nobody has to fight. When you return to your homes you can each send me a postcard and I'll remember this U.N. lunch. It will make me happy." He wrote his name and address for each of us.

Taieb shifted his legs. Behind his head, above the garden wall in the sky swallows were tracing their loops and dives. The white cotton of Taieb's djellabah fell halfway down his bare calves, down to an inch above his pearl-gray socks. The color of the skin of his legs was a reticent mild Arab color like a faded suntan. But where were we going to sleep, he wanted to know. We were coming out into the street and neither Mr. Taieb nor Yves seemed to notice the man with two live chickens slung from his neck, or the child pulling a goat. The next bus for Mr. Taieb's suburb wouldn't leave until four, and in the meantime he could help us find a hotel.

Taieb waited in the entrance hallway while Yves and I followed a bent and larcenous-looking crone to the third floor where we deposited our suitcases in a room that, like all the others we were to have in Tunisia, was spacious and high-ceilinged. It had a window with belled wrought-iron grillwork outside and blue wooden shutters, and beds, and it was clean. When we came back downstairs Mr. Taieb spoke pointedly to the woman in Arabic, advising her, I imagined, that our belongings shouldn't be touched. And then, assured that we had written down the name and address of our hotel, he took his leave. "Remain allies," he said, "with each other and with Tunisia. Enjoy your visit, and when you're back home send me a picture postcard. I'll show them to my wife and my Aisha. Write in French, or even in English I'll know who it's from. I'll say they're from Pompidou and Carter. Aisha reads only Arabic and my wife doesn't read at all. It will make them laugh. I'll say Pompidou and Carter are expressing their admiration for my fig brandy. Well, *au revoir,* my friends, *au revoir.*"

Yves and I agreed that what we needed was a nap and so we went back up to the room and barely had time to take shoes off before collapsing. I woke in shadow and didn't know where I was. Then I heard Yves sleeping quietly, and then I noticed from beyond the shutters a sort of audible tapestry, a *mille fleurs* of little cries. I stood and opened the blue shutters on a yellow sky inscribed with many more swooping and fluttering swallows than I had seen before.

As we walked out in the falling night to find supper, Yves explained that a "sand wind" had yellowed the sky. But surely sand was too heavy? "Yes, but maybe it's very fine, or dust. Anyway that's what the Arabs always said when the sky looked that way. 'Sand wind,' and they would nod."

The next day we toured the souk with its jewelry and rugs, and in the afternoon saw the barbaric ruins of Carthage. The next day we went west to Bizerte to see the apartment building Yves had grown up in, and the Russian church he remembered. The next day we went east to the white and blue village of Sidi bou Said hung like swallows' nests over the blue sea. That afternoon we took a long-distance taxi south down the coast to Gabès, the first leg of a coastal progress that eventually took us on a midnight dhow just large enough for one taxi out to Djerba, Ulysses' island of the lotos-eaters.

In the ten years since, Yves and I have remained allies. He sent Mr. Taieb a card from Toulon but, by the time I'd made my way back to the U.S. and realized I'd misplaced the address, Yves also had let it slip away. I doubt that Mr. Taieb waited for my card, though I know it would have pleased him. Over the years I've tried to let the kindness he showed two strangers replicate itself in me. And while I know his gift was freely given, still I've wished I could keep my promise to him. I keep it now, inadequately, the only way I can:

Taieb ben Khalifa ben Slimane still lives in the Cité Bouchoucha, which isn't the housing development it sounds. It is an oasis village, and a fountain plays in Taieb's walled garden, where he and his wife sit in the fragrant evening listening to bird song or the music from a neighbor's radio. Their Aisha has become a policewoman and was recently assigned to direct traffic at a busy downtown Tunis intersection. One of Taieb's grandchildren has died, but otherwise all is well with his family. Twice a year he still travels by ship to France and he still has luck placing his fig brandy there. In Tunis sometimes he takes a meal at l'Etoile de Nabeul. Lifelong friends may join him, and they talk of those who are absent, and of changes.

Roof Work

1

I'm Patrick Clusel and this is a story about two things that happened to me within a week of each other some eight years ago. The things happened to me but the story is really about other people and not so much about me.

I was twenty, making my living then as now driving tourists in a horse-drawn barouche about the old Québec upper town spring, summer, and fall, plowing snow through the winter, and doing odd jobs year round. At the time I was staying rent-free in an efficiency at the back of the house in the lower town my older sister, Laure, and her husband owned (and still own), putting aside nearly everything I earned. A retired couple down the street, the Van Franks, needed me to replace some broken slate on their back roof that fall. I did it one Saturday while the barouche was in the shop. Mr. Van Frank was alive at the time but only Mrs. Van Frank—Anne, though I didn't call her that then—was home. We went upstairs to their bedroom, whose dormer gave onto the damaged roof. I tied one end of a long rope to their heavy bed and the other end first around my waist and then to my tray of slates and tools. Anne held the tray while I stepped out and then she handed it through to me. The three or four broken slates were only a couple of yards from the window but the pitch was steep enough to make the going slow. I hooked the tray and adjusted it so it was level.

The whole time I was working, Anne stood at the window talking with me. She did most of the talking. She had once taught school and it was easy to see her in front of a class of kids. She talked mainly about herself that afternoon, but I could tell she was doing it for its educational value, not because it was her favorite subject. Some pigeons hoping for a handout settled along the peak of the roof and talked pigeon-talk, and kept their eyes peeled, and didn't clatter away till I stood and walked back to the window. Anne Van Frank herself is small and birdlike, and the dormer she stood in reminded me of a cuckoo clock.

She and her husband supported the separatist Free Québec movement more than anyone else in the neighborhood. They were both feminists too, I think, and Alex, who must have been around eighty, twenty years or so older than Anne, had lately started buttonholing people to air his views about the church. As I told Anne, the week before he'd told me he thought the pope was a living joke.

Anne frowned slightly, with a hint of a blush. She asked if I was a practicing believer. Not at all, I said, although I wouldn't have spoken that way of the pope myself.

Anne said, "No. Well, I hope Alex knew your attitude before he said that. He sometimes can be tactless on the subject. All religion is offensive to him. He scorns it."

She must feel the same way, I supposed.

"Not exactly. I tell Alex he shouldn't get his back up so about it, though I understand. You and your contemporaries would hardly imagine how serious a matter it was for him in his youth."

Not for her?

"Less, I think, and it was different. Alex grew up a Roman Catholic in Belgium but I was born here, up in Jonquière, and my family were Calvinist schismatics, fairly embattled and pious ones. I began to feel uncomfortable about it all at an early age. With my family's congregation the main thing was faith, and they expected various testimonials—loyalty oaths. I'd done it as a matter of course but when I was about twelve I started to dislike saying things about myself I knew to be false, and then in another year or two I stopped saying them."

That must have pleased her family, I guessed.

"They were good people but I'm sure they would have given me a hard time about it. Except that when I finally stopped testifying it happened in a way that didn't leave them much room to object."

How did it happen? Anne didn't pause to go misty-eyed, she was just answering my question as she told about her youth. Replacing broken slates is slow, easy work, and I'd done it before, for other neighbors and for my sister and brother-in-law, so I could listen without difficulty.

"Itinerant clerics refueled us from time to time and it happened when one of them was in Jonquière, the last night. For a week my family and I had gone to our church every evening to hear him preach. He was a nice-looking young man with a magnetic manner, and at my age I was susceptible to that, of course. A part of his format—it was the same each night—was a novelty, at least to me. At the end he asked everyone with a troubled heart, a question or a problem, to kneel at the altar and pray silently for an answer. That much I'd seen before. The novelty was, he insisted that no one come to kneel there without a sincere desire for an answer and, what was more remarkable, that no one leave the altar without having received it.

"The problem could be anything, but the one he talked about most was lack of faith, or doubt. Night after night his line was the same: if you honestly requested assurance or belief you'd get it. Even if you were convinced it wouldn't happen, that didn't matter—it would happen if you wanted it to.

"The first night I was astonished by this. It took about twenty minutes, during which three-quarters of the congregation each walked down to the front, knelt for a few minutes, and then returned to the pews. Not a word was spoken, there were only muffled sustained chords except when the organist did his kneeling, and the creaking of floorboards, and coughs. But the hush over everything was impressive. Because, you see, it was very dramatic. There was no way of knowing when the person beside you might stand and walk away to get the guaranteed answer. I found it electrifying, particularly the first time.

"Through the week I thought about this thing that was happening at the service every night. I've thought about it since. He was a shrewd young fellow, that preacher, if he devised it himself."

"What I was trying to work out that week was, should I accept his proposal. It was such a dilemma that I never knew whether or not I was going to, and at the end of the twenty minutes I couldn't tell whether I was relieved or disappointed that I hadn't.

"By then I was feeling pretty sure it was all baloney, and yet the young man seemed to have some kind of authenticity, some charisma. It wasn't supposed to work unless you really wanted it to, so I had to decide if I did. I couldn't imagine what it would be like to receive a direct message from a deity, but I decided that if such knowledge could be had I did indeed want it and I would be a fool not to. But what if my prediction and not the young preacher's should come true? I could imagine what that would be like—it would be demoralizing. I could imagine returning to my pew knowing I had just played a part in a charade. And although I was beginning to think that my very presence in the pew amounted to support for a charade, still this would have been much more degrading. It would have been like actually casting your vote in a rigged election instead of just watching the victor on television with the rest of your family. It was a bind, as it was intended to be. What would you have done, Patrick?"

I smiled and shook my head. No idea.

"I didn't know what to do either but the more I thought about it the more important it seemed. The last evening I was pretty worried, and when the final twenty-minute period started I was trembling. I must have glanced at my wrist watch thirty times as the first ten minutes ticked past. I've never been able to recall what the thoughts were that flashed through my head before I stood and walked to the altar, but it was like an inspiration. All of a sudden I knew with perfect clarity what I was to do.

"I walked forward to the altar, I knelt and bowed my head and shut my eyes and it was as if all my faculties, all my soul and mind were marshaled into one big plea for a divine response, and one big listening for that response. It was as real and honest as could be—it had to be, you see. I didn't move or open my eyes. I've probably never before or since been so absorbed and concentrated. But at the same time, after a while I was aware that no one but me was left at the altar.

"I don't know exactly how long I stayed there. I think it was only fifteen minutes or so beyond the twenty allotted to that part of the service. There were signs of increasing restlessness. I could hear people clear their throats to remind me that I was inconveniencing them. I noticed that the organist had stopped playing after a while, too. I noticed these things as if in passing and they didn't bother me because there was nothing I could do about them. Because the young preacher had insisted that no one leave the altar without having been answered. And I was carrying out his instructions in the best of faith. I was taking him at his word as they pretended to have done, and I was certainly prepared to stay there much longer than fifteen or twenty extra minutes."

You'd think the congregation would have just gone home, some of them anyway.

"It would have been sensible, wouldn't it? I don't think any of them did though. The ceremony was to close with a benediction and it would have seemed almost an act of insubordination to leave without having been dismissed. Also, despite their impatience I think they were curious about what I was up to. Already it was odd enough and I think they thought something still odder might happen that they wouldn't want to miss. And naturally they must have been thinking, we've put up with her preposterous behavior for ten minutes, it won't hurt to give her another minute or two.

"Our own permanent preacher, who was assisting at the service and who, incidentally, was a good man, must have had some inkling of what was happening and realized that no end was in sight as things stood, because he tiptoed over to me and whispered in my ear. He suggested that I go back and sit down, and he said that he and the young preacher would talk with me after the benediction.

"Now I could simply have ignored him or given him an explanation in case he needed one. Because in a sense I was breaking faith by complying. But the same sort of inspiration I had followed to that point now told me to obey him, and I did. I slipped back to the nearest empty space in the pews, our preacher gave a chastened benediction, and the service was over, and with it the special week."

Up in Jonquière half a century ago, the middle of the Depression, those Calvinist lumbermen and farmers and tradespeople and their families all watching the girl leave the altar. I slid another slate into place. If she hadn't gone back to the pews, maybe the message would have come through. Maybe it was on its way and needed only two minutes more to reach her.

Anne stood in the window with her arms folded, no more smiling than a wren would. "Do you think?"

Maybe there was interference.

"Did you ever pick up such a message, Patrick?"

Never, but then I never really tried.

"Good for you. I never did either afterwards. Twenty-five minutes is enough of a life to waste on it. I knew that, by the end of the benediction. When our preacher and the young itinerant took me to the organ loft and the young one wanted me to try again I declined. I explained it all to them and apologized for having held up the service. Our preacher was thoughtful and subdued but the young fellow let out all the stops. The week had gratified him right up to when I went to the altar, and then at the eleventh hour this bony mite of a girl had rocked the boat. If he'd had a chance to explain me away it wouldn't have rankled so, but the format had precluded that. The format and perhaps also our preacher, who blessed and dismissed the assembly before the young one had a chance to get a last word in edgewise. The young one probably felt like wringing my neck, wouldn't you guess? But the format precluded that too."

"But he was resourceful. People had left the church building and gone home with their impression of the whole week colored by what had just happened. There was no immediate remedy—it wouldn't do for him to follow them and try to put me in my place house by house, and anyway there wasn't time, since he had to be elsewhere on the morrow. But if he could manage to bring me round, if he could sway me there in the organ loft the week might be salvaged because word would seep out that I had seen the light. The week would become a triumph and the very recalcitrance of my case would then count towards his glory. So he let out all the stops he could, given who he was and who I was and the presence and mood of the other cleric, which constrained him.

"He suggested that we kneel together and pray side by side. The seduction probably wouldn't have gone further than that—I don't imagine he'd as much as have laid his hand over my shoulder. But just kneeling side by side with him in the semidarkness there in silence would have been exciting to me, as he well knew. It was tempting but I declined. I said I couldn't see any point in it. So then he switched his tack and tried to intimidate me. He warned me with a simile so peculiar I've remembered it ever since.

"He said that the kingdom of righteousness was like a pendulum. I was supposed to reach out and catch hold when it was near because if I didn't it would swing away without me, out of my reach. He said it would swing back toward me again and I'd have another chance of hopping aboard, and so on for the rest of my life. But he warned me that the pendulum naturally swept out a smaller arc each swing, and therefore I ought to grab it then when it was closer than it ever would be again.

"Well, it was the most ordinary sort of scare tactic—buy now before the prices go up. But the picture his simile presented was peculiar in so many ways I couldn't help wondering about it. He didn't mention devils but I think he must have intended them to be somewhere in the picture."

Somewhere below the pendulum, no? Far enough below so they wouldn't be able to scorch it or jump up onto it.

"Yes, but that would mean I was out of their reach already, as high as the highest point of the pendulum's arc, maybe a little higher. You see how strange it is. But I don't think the young fellow had much considered the implications of his simile.

"Blandishments had rolled off me and now so did intimidations. I had done all I could at the altar before, and the message hadn't reached me—I hadn't been able to reach the pendulum, according to him. However regrettable, it had happened and there was not a thing anyone could do about that."

No sense crying over spilt milk.

"You're a man after my own heart, Patrick. Though the

young preacher didn't so much want me to cry as to pretend it hadn't been spilt. I wouldn't and he must have seen he just wasn't going to succeed with me. It made him very angry but he controlled himself and it only came through in a bit of rudeness. He said he suspected I hadn't really wanted an answer when I knelt at the altar. But I absolutely had. I don't know whether he understood that or not, but he could see I was proof against the accusation and so he left in a huff without saying anything more to me.

"Our permanent preacher had said almost nothing in the loft but before the young fellow left he poured oil on the waters. He was looking at the floor, it was as if he was musing aloud. He said, 'Anne has a profound spirit, I know. I trust that in time she will accept our faith profoundly.' I think he knew I wouldn't—I knew it. But I didn't feel like correcting him then or as he saw me home from the church building or ever after. He was a good man regardless of his profession. Alex of course scoffs when I say that. All the same it's true."

I slid another slate up over its nails and then eased out the wedges I had lifted its two overlappers with. I wondered what became of the young preacher.

"I've no idea. He may well be dead now."

But did Anne mean she knew right then and there that it was all over for religion?

"Yes, I did."

It sounded to me like a load off her mind.

"It put a load on my mind for a while."

On?

"My family and some others in the congregation would have guessed the sort of answer I'd been kneeling at the altar so long for. The congregation and the town—Jonquière was much smaller then—thought of me as a bookish child destined for spinsterhood and schoolteaching—I did teach school for a while, but then I married Alex and stopped. They thought of me as overearnest and a bit wilful, which I was. Mainly though they hadn't thought about me at all. But now they would think about me some because of the altar business. I wondered how they would treat me after it. Would they quiz me? Would they be angry?

"No one in the town, none of my family mentioned it to me. Among themselves though there had been some mention. I knew because with people who hadn't been at the service that night I noticed the same change in attitude toward me as with those who had been: they were polite. No instance of it was at all remarkable but I could feel it a hundred times a day. Everyone had become ever-so-slightly reserved and cautious about me. They were watching me out of the corners of their eyes.

"That guardedness didn't so much bother me. In its way it was flattering, you know. The real trouble was in me, in how I thought about them.

"It was a little like the emperor's new clothes. By my obstinacy at the altar I'd as much as said the emperor was naked whereas they, even though they'd certainly heard me, they wouldn't acknowledge it and they were persisting in the pretense. I couldn't imagine their frame of mind. Not at all. My people, the only people I had known, had always seemed more or less like me, more or less understandable and more or less admirable. Now they seemed none of those and I felt a kind of despair for them. And for myself, lodged among them. It was a hard time to get through."

I asked whether her parents wanted her to continue attending church.

"They asked if I would like to. There'd never been any question before but now they invited me. No, I said at first. I was surprised that they'd suppose I might. But after I'd seen more of how things were I didn't see how it could matter a whit whether I went along with them or not. Because the silence and the distance I felt around me seemed to dwarf considerations of my own integrity. And so sometimes I went along, sometimes not, and for the most whimsical reasons as the mood struck me.

"At first when I went they would grow especially polite and wary, some of them. But as they realized I wasn't going to make any more scenes they relaxed. Eventually the slight guardedness ebbed away from all their dealings with me. They seemed to forget how I had once held them captive from their dinners for fifteen minutes, and they accommodated the one anomalous residue of that evening very well. It was as if since childhood I had been not only a humorless spinster-to-be and so forth but also one who missed religious services often as not. Who knows, in time I myself might have come to believe it if I'd stayed there.

"But I wasn't forgetting anywhere near as fast as they seemed to be doing. I found them strange and a little contemptible even when they seemed to have reincorporated me entirely and for some time after. It wasn't very pleasant, Patrick. It was a weight on my mind."

"But I got past it. I came away, for one thing. I met people who didn't seem so fraudulent—some, including Alex, who seemed no more fraudulent than I did. That was liberating. I had fun and work, good medicine the both. Then a member of my family died and I went back for the funeral. It was someone I and most of the town loved. I think the experience sobered me. I think I saw that I had been naïve to take preachers at their word. In and of itself, the apparatus of the religion—what the townspeople believed or pretended to believe about messages from a deity, for instance—was a patent fraud. Yet with them at least it seemed a harmless, even good, fraud. It didn't even quite seem a fraud any more. It seemed as if it might be a figure for some truth. Because somehow it was consoling some of the people in a way no such flimsy lie as I had taken it to be could have done. It seemed to me that many of them saw the flimsiness and the falsehood quite as clearly as I did.

"I thought more about it after I left. I began to be surprised at how patient they had been with me before. If the emperor weren't naked, talk of his clothes would be merely that, and there wouldn't be much reason for it. But since he was naked as a jaybird for all to see, when you talked of his new clothes you couldn't fool anybody and you weren't trying to. You were trying to talk about something altogether different and you were probably trying to tell the truth about it. It must not be easy. When a pubescent child in the crowd squeaks out, 'I don't see any clothes on him,' she must seem either perverse or awfully simple-minded. I suppose the best you can do is tell her, 'Ssh.' Because you'll adhere to the fiction if its real subject is important enough and if you seem to be telling the truth about it. You say, 'Ssh' or just ignore her. You hope she won't distract you again. If she keeps quiet and watches what's going on, she may even come to understand what it is you're up to. You hope for that too.

"Alex disagrees. He thinks no dealing is falsehood should be countenanced. He objects not to the shame or dishonor that made me pipe up but to the danger. It certainly can be dangerous. Do you know what I'm thinking of?"

It could be dangerous if you forget that it's not true, that it's a code for something else.

"Why is that dangerous?"

Well, in Anne's case in the church, she might have crippled herself kneeling.

"And crippled anybody else who was making the same mistake and waiting for me to move. You're right, Patrick. And it's dangerous in other ways. It can be dangerous even if you don't make that mistake."

How so, I asked, as I made room for the last slate to slip into place.

"At my relative's funeral the fiction was working properly, I think. I knew that and yet I knew full well that that particular fiction—Christianity, I mean—had a long history of working very badly indeed. Some of its evil did come from people's having made the mistake of taking it for the truth it was only a code or figure for. But I think such literal-mindedness accounts more for the folly than for the evil. Because so far as I remember, the religion itself doesn't contain too many counsels to wrongdoing. And yet its professors have done enormous amounts of many kinds of wrong and harm, and they've sanctioned those wrongs and harms with the religion, even though it itself contains explicit counsels against some of them. It says that its god says not to kill people, for instance. So I don't think many of its professors have ever taken it very literally.

"But if it's possible to tell each other real truths by talking about the emperor's clothes, it must also be possible to tell each other real falsehoods that way too. That's the danger I was thinking of. And knowing which is which may not be easy. With the Christian fiction, it seems to have been close to impossible."

"So I agree with Alex that dealing in patent falsehoods is dangerous. But I don't think it's as pernicious as he does. I'm more inclined now to see it as like some powerful machine, say an electric lawnmower. It's more hazardous than an ordinary lawnmower, if it's working badly. But if it's working well you may be able to do a job faster with it. It may even enable you to cut grass you simply couldn't with an ordinary mower. Something like that. I wish Alex could see it that way.

"Where did you learn slate roofing, by the way, Patrick? You seem expert."

Hardly, but this should stop the leaks. It's the kind of thing you just pick up, really. The first time I did it must have been back in Trois Rivières with my father.

"Is he still there?"

I laid the tools and the last broken slate in the tray. Yes, my father is still in Trois Rivières. He's in the cemetery. My mother too—she died when I was a baby. My father was killed in an automobile accident three years back. Nobody at fault. It was raining and there was a blowout, skidding. The driver of the other car got off with a broken arm. Some machines are more hazardous than others.

I stood and the pigeons flapped away. Anne blinked.

"Times like that, Patrick, as a rule the emperor's new clothes come out of the wardrobe."

I stepped gingerly up to the window. There was a requiem mass for Poppa, the only one I remember ever going to. His sisters and brother took care of everything. I think they and their families have stayed with the church, but Poppa, as far back as I can remember, was pretty well lapsed. The accident's why I came here for my last year of school—Laure and her husband had the vacant efficiency. I handed the tray through the window and stepped over the sill. As I unhitched myself and the tray from the bedstead, Anne walked to the dresser for her purse. No, I said, it's on the house. She had provided the slates and, as for the little labor, her story had more than reimbursed me. She shook her head and started to protest, but she was studying my face and she changed her mind. Downstairs on her doorstep, she held out her small hand to me.

2

Four days later the carriage was ready to roll, and my piebald gelding and I had a profitable Wednesday showing Old Québec to tourists. I stabled him around six and took a bus out to a cut-rate electronics outlet in the new town to pick up a tuner and amplifier kit. After dinner my friend Hammed came over and we assembled it.

Hammed wasn't a real friend but he was the closest thing to it I had. Even back in Trois Rivières before Poppa died, I'd been a bit of a loner. I was always cheerful and outgoing—

you had to be to make anything driving the barouche—and I liked talking with most anybody for a while, but I just didn't seem cut out for close friendships. People who knew me didn't mind.

Hammed was a naturalized Tunisian. His family had come to Québec the year before I moved here. He brought some kif along and we smoked it as we assembled the equipment and then listened to its performance. Between us we had more than adequate knowledge of the basic electronics. The sound was good even discounting the enhancement of the kif, and most of the old background noise had dropped away. Hammed left around eleven-thirty to catch a bus back to his family's high rise in the new town. Residual effects of his African dope, together with a kind of echo of my rooftop talk with Mrs. Van Frank, and the fatigue of an unusually full day, must have contributed to something that happened an hour or so later.

Hammed and I had listened to Claude Léveillée and Gilles Vigneault sing Québec songs, and then I'd heard a Tschaikovsky piano concerto and then one side of a record of whale songs as I drank a cup of instant hot chocolate. Then I kicked off my shoes and lay on my day bed for an indeterminate period. I was doing that kind of thoughtless thought near sleep you never remember—little pictures, little thoughts coming and going, with a heightened sense of touch along the rims of my eyelids.

Then out of nowhere like a shock came an image of my father's rotted face, close and physical. Immediately the image changed into its memory, variable and fading and vivid. All this was quick, and the memory had become its own memory before the shock registered in my heart and pulse. When that came it was like a reembodiment for me out of a presence diffused around the patient face. My eyelids retracted to the maximum and I raised myself to a half-crouch on the day bed, not to fight or flee, but because I was in a pure free state of extreme alertness. By then the compounding memory was changing into knowledge.

The night in Trois Rivières at the house when the highway patrolman woke me to inform me of Poppa's death I had gone kind of gruff, wiping away the tears like sweat during a hard day's work in the sun. Coming to terms with it was hard for Laure even though she was already married and living in Québec, and it was sure hard for me. We had drawn together, and got through it. Poppa's death had been on my mind like a big fact to be coped with during the move to Québec and all. It meant, for instance, that I reviewed what I knew of his goodness and tried to keep it from going to waste by fostering what I could of it in myself—though that was tricky because people would then want to give me the credit. Anyway, by now Poppa didn't seem so much on my mind. The fact that he wasn't alive had come be be just a fact, no more to be coped with than the fact that my mother wasn't either.

I fell out of the crouch into a rag-doll collapse, my back against the wall, to think over what I had just seen. Three phrases I still remember passed through my mind: "The most important thing. Him not me. All this time."

The mental shorthand meant that the sight of Poppa's face, his rotted face, made a mockery of all my coping, because not once since the accident had I been sensible of what the vision now forced me to reckon with. When the officer had first told me about it I had shed tears but even those first tears were from grief at losing Poppa. Similarly, what I had come to terms with wasn't really the fact that he was dead but rather the fact that he wasn't living, which soon became the fact that I was without a living parent. But all this time Poppa himself had been dead, his body had been decomposing all the while I had been trying to deal with the loss, Laure's and my loss. From the start, and increasingly, I had taken the death as a fact about me (which it was) and strangely not taken it as what it was above all, a fact about Poppa, his the face half-gone by now. None of which had a thing to do with me or me with it—there my grief or coping counted for nothing.

I felt ashamed of having occupied myself with something so remote from the main truth as how the death bore on me. Not exactly because I had dishonored my father or been remiss. Maybe I had, but in his being dead nothing I might do mattered. It was rather that my mind seemed to have been small. I undressed, brushed my teeth, peed, and turned the lights out.

It was raining the next morning when I awoke, a cold steady autumn rain the Van Franks would be glad to have their roof repaired against. The barouche has an accordion roof I can pull up in a shower, but I knew no visitors would be looking for a horse-drawn tour in that weather, so I spent the morning doing some more testing and adjusting of the new sound system, and thinking over what had happened to me the night before.

My assessment of it was more or less the same except that it didn't seem at all strange now. It had happened last night but it could as well have happened months before, it seemed so settled in my mind. It had become something to think about and generalize from. For instance, mightn't it be that somehow with living people I made the same kind of mistake I'd been making with Poppa the past three years? What would that mean? Well, I supposed it would mean coping and coming to terms with them from my standpoint until a corresponding vision of a living face finally alerted me. I tried to imagine what that would be like, with Laure, or with Hammed, say, or with Mrs. Van Frank, a vision out of the blue or even actually seeing the person in a way that disembodied me. I couldn't quite imagine it, though I felt (and still do) that something like that could happen one day. I decided to compliment Hammed on his kif the next time I saw him, even though I knew the real catalyst had been Anne Van Frank's story.

Basse Ville

It was sunshiny but cold out on the river in the wind on the open deck of the ferry returning to Québec from Lévis one afternoon seven or eight years ago, going on four o'clock, September. The customs house where the ferry would dock looked derelict and the sight of it made the wind sweeping down the river feel even colder. Toward the middle of the crossing, passengers who had strolled on the outer deck retreated to the glassed-in promenades. But one passenger stayed out in the wind through the whole crossing—an old, squat red-nosed man in a tatterdemalion greatcoat, me, name of Alex Van Frank, not minding the wind one bit (too tough) on my way back from seeing my daughter Ida and son-in-law Sammy.

I was half Sammy's age with twice his I.Q. and more experience of the world than he'll ever get when I first set foot in this damn country. I started oil painting at the age of eighty-one and in eighteen months and a few days I've painted more than a hundred pictures. Those paintings will be worth a lot of money when I kick the bucket. I've given only two or three away—the rest are home, some framed in our dining room and the others wrapped in waxed paper under the bed. Anne'll be rich—they're better than any life insurance I could afford.

I'm leaving everything to her even though I probably should set a few paintings aside for Ida and Sammy because who knows, Anne might lose her mind or leave everything to charity. But what the hell. It's only money, let her do what she wants.

In 1932 Alex sailed from Ostend to Québec with high hopes for the new world. From childhood he had been destined for the priesthood but scarcely had he begun to read Descartes and then other subversives, especially Spinoza, when he underwent a change of heart. "The pope has to take a shit just like everybody else does," is how he summarized his new sentiments to fellow students in coffeehouses. When he left the university, his father disowned him. He found work as a cobbler's assistant and lived frugally for two years in Louvain. An acquaintance who had emigrated to Québec wrote that socialism was on the doorstep of the Americas, and people were saying the same thing in Louvain newspapers and coffeehouses. Alex believed them enough to decline buying a pension when he came to Québec.

Socialism dragged its feet but Alex liked Québec anyway. He signed on with a shipping firm and traveled up and down the St. Lawrence, up and down the Atlantic seaboard, to the Orient, off and on thirty-five years for the company. Through the war he served as ship's engineer dodging U-boats in the North Atlantic to provision the Allies. He was no wild-eyed revolutionary, but he continued to believe that economic inequality was an evil and a shame. During the late thirties, when once again socialism seemed to have a chance in the New World, he attended various rallies and at one of them in Québec he met Anne, a native Québecoise twenty years younger than he. They married.

Anne was a schoolteacher. She had left her parents' farm in the north and come to the city to make her own living. Now she abandoned her profession for full-time housekeeping and motherhood. She and Alex bought two adjoining houses in the lower town, all their savings going for the down payment. In three decades the houses were paid for. Alex and Anne stayed in the smaller—after Ida was born they talked of changing and it might have been sensible, but by then they knew how each square meter of the floor sloped. They rented the adjoining house to a series of tenants over the years.

Thooo-oog. Thoog. The ferry slowed until without any perceptible moment of contact it had berthed and gangplanks were being lowered.

Over the years Alex made good use of his knowledge of cobbling. His work was coarse, not for Anne's shoes but okay for his own, like these in which he descended the gangplank among the last passengers in a splay-footed sashay step by step through the shelter where others waited to board, out into the open space with dogs and pedestrians and a few parked cars. There was less wind. Over the dark customs house stood the evening star.

It was the same celestial object as the morning star and not a star at all, but Venus. In a thrift shop Alex had found a book about the universe with many pictures and diagrams. He had read the entire book ostensibly browsing in the course of several visits to the shop, and then he had bought and reread it. Some stars are so dense that gravity holds back their very light, he informed Anne, even though such a fact rolled off her like water off a duck. What the hell, wonders of the universe probably only matter to you if you're about to kick off, so maybe it's all to the good for your wife not to bat an eye at them.

Alex could walk a long distance but he went slowly and often had to stop to rest on a low wall or a bench. It was in these rests that this apparently genial little man who looked like the father of his favorite painter Rembrandt would be seized by anger he could barely contain. There was no knowing what he might find himself remembering. It could as easily be something he hadn't thought of in decades—gathering eggs winter mornings in his boyhood—as it could a frequently recalled event like his and Anne's wedding night. The recollection had a life of its own, and it seemed the most natural thing in the world while it lasted. During these rests also Alex was prone to hallucinate as he sat with his hands on his knees, the sun in his face. He might smell rope or jasmine, a long vista might open in the shrubbery or a face move back and forth there to say no. Or so it seemed: half an hour later he couldn't be sure whether it had happened or not and by evening he would have forgotten it.

Alex proceeded along one of the narrow streets of the lower town and turned right into Cleroux Street, the cul-de-sac where he and Anne and their new tenants the Schumanns lived. Alex tipped his hat to his young neighbor Laure Poujade, who sketched tourists in the upper town. She was okay, not like those wild teenagers on their motorbikes who tried to run you over in the upper town, and lately had once even roared up and down Cleroux. Alex had given them what for, and stepped off the curb so they had to veer around him, and the one in black leather had nicely scuffed the elbow of his jacket when his machine skidded out from under him. But what if they ever tried it again? Alex scowled, and scowled more at the flower boxes in Mr. Catanese's windows, which practically blocked the sidewalk. Well before that obstruction Alex crossed to his house.

He shut the door behind him. If those ungoverned youths continued to appear on their motorbikes, wouldn't it be necessary to lock doors? Might as well move south of the border and get murdered right away. He hung up his coat and blew his nose. "Anne?" The air was cool and still. "Anne?"

"Cogito!" came a cry from the dining room. *"Cogito! Ergo sum!"* The bright insistent voice was not Anne's but that of Alex's

parrot, Sinbad. "Shut up," Alex muttered. Anne should be home at this hour. Alex frowned.

Sinbad moved sideways on the bar he spent most of his hours on, to have a better view of the doorway Alex was coming through. Alex had bought him when he was less than a year old, almost thirty years before in what is now the Malagasy Republic. The sea voyage to Canada had been like the movement of a branch in the wind repeated ad nauseam. Since then he had lived here in Cleroux Street. Sinbad was large, strong, and beautiful. Though he had not flown since '47, he kept his wings and tail preened. He would outlive Alex by many years, and possibly when that little man, who had shortened and thickened over the years as his schnoz reddened and swelled and lumped up, when he was in the ground there might be reason to have one's flying feathers in trim.

The insistence with which Sinbad proclaimed that he thought and therefore was had nothing to do with the expressed claim. He used the same tone for everything Alex had made him learn: it was the tone Alex had used to insist that he con the phrase.

Alex was starting to glower. Where was Anne who should be home at this hour? Sinbad turned a cool eye on him, muttered, "What the hell," and blinked.

Alex half-suspected that Anne was keeping a rendezvous with the dapper young instructor of the social dances held Saturday afternoons at the senior citizens' center and attended assiduously by Anne in the face of Alex's scoffs. In fact she was clip-clopping down the Breakneck Steps to the lower town in her sensible black shoes, on her way back from the post office, and minutes later she was in the house slipping off her flowered scarf and telling Alex how she had given the postal worker a piece of her mind. "I asked him why we should paste the queen's face on our letters. I think it was educational for them to hear somebody speak up." Anne smoothed her white blouse and khaki skirt, the clothes she wore in Alex's portrait of her.

Anne was birdlike (though not much like Sinbad), fine-boned and discreet. In the twenty-by-thirty-centimeter painting, which hung with fifteen others the same size above the sideboard in the dining room, she was taking an afternoon nap, hands under her cheek. Her blouse had become pink and the twill skirt a robin's-egg blue, and her shoes sat side by side on the floor. You could see that her eyes were closed and that her hair was short and gray, but little more than that in the tiny face. This was the only painting Alex had yet attempted from life. And, while it might not enable you to distinguish Anne among other petite gray-haired women, it was one of Alex's best works. Inspiration would be the simplest explanation for his having chosen to show Anne asleep. She did take the occasional afternoon nap, but when she was awake you only needed observe her a short time to know how hard it was to imagine her asleep, and so appreciate how Alex's imagination had zeroed in.

René Catanese had no idea his window boxes occasioned grumbling. He didn't suppose his neighbors might think anything at all about his window boxes or, for that matter, about him. His legal residence was in the upper town and, though he had come to spend nearly all his time down in the narrow building with geraniums, still in his mind it remained an office where he managed the Québec Orient Company.

At one time the company had swayed the governments of Canada and of some Chinese provinces, but the Chinese revolution had accelerated a decline already in progress. From the beginning René had managed the moribund company as a diversion, looking in from time to time before returning to what he called his work or, for a brief time later, to his wife. His work was amateur botany, "amateur" not because desultory but because he did it out of a disinterested love.

René let this work he loved direct him and when it pointed straight at succulents he followed without cadging. For Québec it was about as ill-chosen as could be but the point was that René hadn't chosen it, he had followed it, around the world in tropical deserts to find new species. He named them for people who had helped him, and then for his wife. When he married her he was in his midthirties and could not imagine being happier. They had the house off the Grande Allée and a cottage on Prince Edward Island, she accompanied him into the desert or he went alone and came back to her. The beatitude was deepening and widening and promising a long future when near their third wedding anniversary she died.

She was in no pain and there had been a lightness in the last weeks, her cues for the tone, champagne in the morning, and for a while after she was gone forever René held the wondering lightness she had found, in which the truth that she was dying and then that she had died could be seen so clearly that there was no cause to dwell on it. Then the lightness had broken. He tried to think his way back, but there was no shelter from the desolation that used him brutally for a long time with no relief in sight.

But eventually that too had come to be over and done with. He was not old yet and it was time to recommence his work. He went down to the Yucatan for samples but back in Québec he realized that his heart hadn't quite been in the expedition. He stopped by the Québec Orient and chatted with the secretary. René was mounting the steps to the upper town when it occurred to him that a window box of geraniums would be good for the office. From then on he took an increasing interest in the company, its history, the rare current business and the comfortable office. He let the succulent work slide some but he didn't abandon it. He built a small greenhouse behind the office. In the upper town he would have used a builder but down here it seemed right to give the work to neighbors or their people, so he had hired Patrick Clusel from up the street to build the structure for him in a corner where it would get afternoon sun. In the upper town if a new floorboard had given way he would have asked the builder for explanation and repair, but down here it seemed better to move something over the hole when he thought about it and say nothing. Some of the boards had developed dry rot anyway, so next summer Patrick could install a whole new floor. René fitted out a bedroom on the second floor of the company building and slept there more often than in the upper town.

He was a large man with coal-black hair that had receded from his high brow. His face was like a Roman senator's, heavy and distinguished, with flat vertical cheeks and pendulous earlobes. He sat patiently at his rolltop desk in the dim office. There was a shaded lamp and beside it a humidor, an ivory puzzle, and a letter opener. Behind glass in bookcases along two walls stood company records, botanical journals, histories, dictionaries, grammars, dog-eared catalogues of porcelain, jade, and other goods the company had traded in, marine atlases bound in green morocco embossed with the company's initials, and desert notebooks of laid vellum covered with René's blunt, even script and graceful line drawings of plants.

You get old and your mind feels like a garbage bag. Sometimes more and more of what Alex Van Frank had stuffed in over eighty-two years was turning out to be garbage—not to mention the crap that had found its way in without ever looking like anything different. It makes thinking harder when it feels that way. It isn't senility—what it is is that there doesn't seem room to turn around in, never mind make noble strides. So be it, what the hell.

Indian summer ended toward early October. It might get down to freezing some nights. When a temperate day came along Alex went out into it for a walk. Anne was over in Lévis keeping an eye on the grandchildren. Sammy and Ida had gone to Montréal to look for a new television set with color. Anne would give Sammy the interesting article on the universe Alex had found in a *National Geographic*. Sammy could read it and then give it back. Maybe he'd have something to say about it. It might make him think, the blankety-blank overgrown boy. He might read it.

Woolen trousers, two moth-eaten cardigans over a shirt and Sammy's old canvas golf hat were all Alex needed to defy the worst a tame air like today's could do, and his horny wide splay feet were shod in his own creations. He lit up a black stogie.

Alex suspected that Julien Schumann was a backstairs Lothario not to be trusted alone with Anne. Alex guessed just from the way the guy looked that his own wife wasn't enough for him. He ran a bookstore in the upper town. He looked about as bookish as a monkey. Hate literature is what Alex guessed Schumann was selling under the counter in his store, or he might be forming a religious sect for loonies.

Otherwise though Alex thought Julien was okay, and he saluted him with good cheer when he saw him in the street. "How'd you like the kick in the pants they gave the pope in Italy?"

"Birth control no less. I wouldn't have expected it," said Julien.

"Ha! I'd like to have seen the look on his face when he opened the paper the next morning. I wonder if he forgot who he was and said goddamn. They probably bring him the paper on a silver platter. Ha, ha, I'd like to have been there."

Julien smiled. "Did you ever see a pope in the flesh?"

Alex said, "I wouldn't sully my eyes," and took a puff of his stogie. "Any trouble with the house? If your rent's not in on time I'll call the police and have you evicted."

Julien smiled. "I'll remember."

Alex chuckled and bade him good day. He could forget his designs on Anne. He seemed brighter than Sammy—Alex enjoyed talking with him whatever his so-called bookstore was a front for. Anne's out of his league though. A Lothario worth his salt ought to be able to see that, no matter how tall he was.

Alex turned and shaded his eyes to look up at the cliff. There it was, the "American Gibraltar." Tourists gaped, inhabitants hardly looked at it. To Alex, gaping seemed the more absurd of the two though he knew that he must have gaped when he saw the rock for the first time as a boy fresh over from Ostend. It was a big rock for a city, and big compared to Alex, but pretty small potatoes compared to the universe. Alex shrugged. He looked from the top down the face of the precipice, and he had a fleeting hallucination of a smile on the rock as his gaze descended.

Then he saw Sinbad his parrot on the front of the second house from the corner hobbling along the cornice at the level of the upper floor, clear as anything. "Malarky," muttered Alex. He looked away at something else. When he looked back—he couldn't resist—Sinbad was gone and a pigeon was alighting where he had been. Puffing his stogie, Alex watched until the pigeon had made its landing. Then he resumed his promenade.

He splurged a quarter on the escalator up to the Place d'Armes. In the upper town people went about their business in larger numbers and with more of a bustle on some of the streets. Others were as quiet as Cleroux Street. Alex stopped in at an Indian shop to peruse some watercolors a Cree inspired by tribal legends had painted. They were selling at forty dollars apiece. After a judicious appraisal Alex decided they weren't bad even though they were nothing like Rembrandt. Anyway what mattered was that people buy them. Like the rich dame who came in fiddling with her purse as Alex left. She disregarded his appearance with gracious tolerance. "Your shit stinks as much as mine," thought Alex as he tipped his hat. "Shabby creature," she must've been thinking. So be it.

Alex spent the noon hour on a park bench with a hard-boiled egg he'd brought in his pocket and a soft drink he'd picked up on the way. It was a sunny park where Alex had first ventured to hold Anne's hand years and years before, and that wasn't the only good idea he'd had here, taking his rest in different seasons. This noon no especially good idea came to him. It had to be that way sometimes too.

The November vandalism in René Catanese's greenhouse occurred during the night or early morning. Around noon when he went out to pot some cuttings an ugly sight awaited him. The shattered pots in the southeast corner could be replaced, and succulents survive root exposure, but plants had been butchered, large ones it had taken years to raise hacked and gouged. One of these wouldn't survive as it stood and the only thing for it was to finish the butchery, divide it into pieces and start again. Nausea and something like panic washed over René. In the hot dry air he broke into a cold sweat looking at this destruction, and he wiped his brow with the back of a hand. He spent the day dressing the green and gray wounds. Absurd as it was, from time to time as he worked he thought he heard a movement behind him and his skin prickled. The next day he had the Clusel boy install a lock on the greenhouse door.

On the surface the incident looked like the kind of random violence cities seemed to be fostering more and more as the century wore on. Outbreaks of it were less common in Canada than south of the border, rarer in Québec than in most other Canadian cities, far rarer in the old town than in the suburbs, and rarest of all in the quiet streets of the lower town. If it was that sort of violence it would be nearly unprecedented, and alarming. If on the other hand it was some malice directed specifically at René, so far as he knew it was entirely unprecedented. Yet in some ways it did seem personal. Nothing else on the premises had been attacked nor apparently anything else in the street. How likely was it that someone destroying randomly would choose something so dear to René as the succulents?

If personal malice did figure, it would seem to follow that the culprit was a fellow botanist or, failing that, one of his neighbors. The first hypothesis seemed ludicrous but the second was worse because of the suspicion it could infect his daily life with. As when old Pascale Mackenzie next door sweeping her stoop bade him good morning and he listened for a hint of mischief or craziness in her voice. Or when, watching the Clusel boy install the lock, it occurred to him that, motives aside, no one in the street looked as capable of the vandalism as Patrick. Who, if he was the culprit, must be enjoying the irony of being paid to install the lock. Which he alone besides René knew how to operate, so he would give himself away should he be mad enough to return for another bout of destruction. Such were the disquieting trains of thought René found himself giving way to.

After the Van Franks had their roof repaired, Anne moved the clothes hamper away from the door where it had stood as a nuisance ever since the roof started to leak in the spring, back to its place in the far corner. The next day while she was out Alex moved it back near the door. Anne reminded him that it had stood in the corner ten years at least, and that in any case she should be able to have it where she pleased since she did the laundry. Alex scowled and reminded her that his earnings had enabled them to buy this and the other house, and said sarcastically that if washing clothes was crippling her he could assume the responsibility. Anne was tempted to accept his offer, her nerves were so frazzled by his new arbitrariness. He gave the hamper a kick that sent it back toward its corner and then stalked in his shambling way out of the room.

Anne couldn't ignore the possibility that she was seeing him go senile. After a moment she pushed the hamper the rest of the way into its corner.

Alex was surly and querulous by turns, resentful, forgetful, arbitrary and, as if that weren't enough, suspicious. That was the most grievous part of it for Anne, his seeming to suspect even her of impossible motives and deeds. With a start she guessed that he thought her responsible for Sinbad's disappearance. She had been over in Lévis with Ida and Sammy's children when the parrot vanished, but facts seemed to count for nothing in Alex's present mood and in any case trotting them out was too saddening. Nor, until such a time as she might know he suspected her, did she want to risk implanting suspicion by a denial. She recalled how she had found him sitting under his reading light that evening. She had supposed that something in the Spinoza open in his lap had moved him to tears. She had hung up her coat and hat, noticed the empty cage and asked where Sinbad was. "Ahhh the sonofabitch is gone," Alex had said with a snuffling laugh and a shake of his head. Anne did fear he thought she'd done it herself or arranged it.

Some groups of a few hundred snowflakes had fallen from nowhere all by themselves like lint shook out a casement above, but the first snow you'd call a snow started after midnight on December eleventh, the day Alex took a painting to the museum. Sinbad was gone all right, a fortnight already. There were no clues Alex could find. Not a soul answered his ad in the newspaper's lost-and-found though he offered a reward. At one time or another Alex suspected everyone in the street including his own wife Anne—why not? somebody had to have done it. He intended to be magnanimous, forget the whole thing as soon as the culprit came forward and made a clean breast. But there wasn't a peep out of the culprit.

Maybe Alex did cry when he first found the bird gone. Maybe blubbering made him feel unworthy to expect help from Spinoza, too. All the same, life goes on. So what: Sinbad was never anything but a parrot. He could've been a human being and life would still go on. Bigwigs think they're indispensable, and con little wigs into half-believing it. But the pope could choke on frog's legs tonight and even if a dozen presidents, sheiks, and the like met their appropriate ends tomorrow dawn we could still enjoy our breakfasts. We could boot out any or all their highnesses like the Shah of Iran. Close their Swiss bank accounts and put them on an island where they could spend the rest of their lives trying to impress one another. They could institute solemnity contests, award a coconut hat to the highness who made other highnesses clam up and quake best. We could bug the island with TV cameras and tune in for a laugh when we didn't have something better to watch.

Alex grinned. He was in bed under three quilts, in his flannel nightshirt. Anne was downstairs reading. Alex turned off his bedside lamp and looked through the window to see if snow had started.

It had been a busy day, up and down the Breakneck Steps twice. In the morning he'd gone up to the art supply store for some turp and a few more canvas boards. As always, he browsed awhile examining supplies in a kind of trance. He was deciding as he nearly always did to resist the temptation to buy this or that luscious tube of a hue he should after all be able to make out of primaries when young Laure Poujade greeted him. "I didn't know you painted, Mr. Van Frank."

"Thought you was the only artist in the street, eh?" Game for ribbing she was and not at all hard on the eyes in her bloom.

Laure had heard about Sinbad's disappearance. When Alex told her he'd given up hope of finding any leads, she suggested buying another parrot.

Alex had already thought of doing that and rejected it as

beneath his dignity. But Laure made it sound so right that now upon leaving her he reconsidered. He went so far as to maneuver himself into a phone booth for the first time ever—and the last, he vowed—to consult yellow pages under "Parrots," "Birds," "Animals," and finally "Pets." Odd a designation for a parrot as that was, the store listed there seemed the best bet, and it was just around the corner. Before extricating himself from the booth, Alex rang up the rescue league he'd found under "Animal." A brisk helpful voice answered.

"Good morning," said Alex. "You take care of lost animals?"

"Yes, if they're found and brought in. Have you found an animal?"

"Me? No. Me, I lost one."

"Oh dear, too bad. We may have it though. Could you describe the animal?"

"A big parrot," Alex began. "He . . ."

"Sinbad?" interrupted the voice.

This was downright startling. "You mean *you* have him?"

"If we did, you'd be the first to know. Sorry. Good-bye."

"Hold the show!" roared Alex. "How the hell do you know my parrot's goddamn name?"

In the street patient automobiles moved, slowed to a stop, began moving. A couple of hippies were slipping off their backpacks beside the phone booth.

"I'm a citizen," Alex said.

The traffic advanced like an accordion, closing as it slowed to a pause, fanning out again when it moved.

"A taxpayer."

The voice at the other end said, "You must not be the party who's made such a . . . who's inquired so repeatedly about this Sinbad. One moment."

The hippies were sitting on the curb smiling at Alex to let him know they wanted the phone. A new voice came on to say that Alex must be the Mr. Van Frank whose wife he ought to thank for her concern over his pet's loss inasmuch as she had been calling the league more often than was necessary. "Okay," said Alex. He worked his way out of the booth—the smiling couple was welcome to it.

The pet store was like a miniature zoo. Had Alex known of it, he'd already have been dropping in from time to time. They had two parrots, neither nearly so handsome as Sinbad. Still, it wouldn't hurt to ask the price, off-handedly so as not to get rooked. The answer sounded like a joke: either of those mediocre birds was selling for almost a thousand times what Sinbad had cost.

Anne was out when Alex came home. He thought about her as he ate lunch at the kitchen table—soup, bread, cider, half a pear. So she'd been making a nuisance of herself in his behalf. He thought about what he had learned at the pet store too. It made sense for somebody to have swiped Sinbad if he was worth such a bundle after all. So.

Then, when Alex was upstairs unwrapping his canvas boards, a plan jelled out of the morning. Laure Poujade was right, he should have a new parrot. More important, he was ashamed about Anne's having borne the brunt of his recent bad moods—Anne of all people—and he should make it up to her with an apology and a gift like an electric typewriter to replace her old manual one. Wherewithal for typewriter and parrot was the crux of the matter. Which he could get by selling one of his paintings. One wouldn't hurt—there'd be plenty for Anne to get rich on after he kicked off.

Selecting the painting was like choosing one of your children to sell into slavery. On the other hand, since Alex didn't know who Québec's richest art patrons might be, he had decided to let the university museum make the purchase and he would be able to step in for a look whenever he wanted. He chose a view of "the most perfect of the northern medieval towns of Europe," Bruges. He had copied it mostly from a black-and-white magazine illustration, replacing the grays with bright pastels, and he had added a vegetable vendor with carrots, leeks, and radishes. Alex wrapped the painting in waxed paper and went up to the museum.

The director couldn't have been over forty. He was standing at a window looking out at something in the courtyard below and he must've thought Alex was his secretary because Alex had come all the way across the room to the big empty desk before the man turned and took in Alex and doubtless the secretary signaling from the doorway. "Yes?"

Alex chuckled. He laid the package on the desk, opened it and stepped back. "Don't be scared, have a look."

With a puzzled smile the man came to his desk and looked at the painting. The smile drained away.

Alex laughed. "Don't worry if you think you can't afford it. We'll say five hundred—call it my charity to Québec."

The museum director inhaled. "Where did you learn to paint, sir?"

Alex beamed. "Self-taught!"

The museum director started to say one thing and then thought better of it. "No . . ." he began, "I'm sorry to disappoint you but no, we won't buy this piece. Whatever the price. So now good day."

Alex shook his head.

"Miss Philippe," said the director, "is there a guard nearby?"

"Okay," Alex said. "Okay then." He folded the paper over the bright panel, tucked the package under his arm, tipped his hat and strolled past Miss Philippe, out into the wintry afternoon, and home.

But the joke was on the museum director. Because Alex would have to have been born yesterday to have really believed they'd buy his painting—wait till you're pushing up daisies, the guy might as well have said. Alex had known it then as well as he knew it now under his quilts. He could see out his window that snow should start soon. He wondered if it might be possible to raise Schumann's rent long enough to supply the money he needed without Anne's getting wind of it.

The parrot Sinbad had been released by a mischief-maker, while Alex was outside talking of the pope with Julien Schumann, and Anne was in Lévis. The person slipped into the house from the back and, when he saw the birdcage, was inspired to undo the latch Sinbad himself had pecked at on occasion over the years.

What was up? Blamed if Sinbad could say. Many another bird's heart would have quailed. Sinbad clambered into his cage's doorway. Perched there, head cocked to one side, he regarded the stranger in its scuffed motorcycle jacket. Sinbad wasn't frightened: although the person radiated no affection like Alex's, it didn't seem to mean him harm. It was in a hurry for him to do something, though. Could it be that old short Alex's time had come? Like a good bird, Sinbad jumped out the cage doorway. He barely had time to half-open his wings before he landed on the rug.

The stranger closed the cage door and then with small movements made it clear that Sinbad wasn't to walk anywhere but across the clean rugs and wood into the hallway and up the stairs. Sinbad took them one at a time. Midway in the climb when he rested a minute, with a glance over his shoulder he saw that the stranger was not far behind, insistent and wordless, with a bluish aura around it. Couldn't have been less like Alex.

Sinbad had never been upstairs. It all looked interesting and, but for the stranger, he could have explored every room. As it was, not knowing how much time there was, he made a U-turn at the banister and went straight to the far end of the corridor, observing as much as he could along the way. At the end he climbed up a bentwood chair and stepped from atop it through a bright hole in the wall onto a ledge. He could see the entire street. Wasn't that old Alex at the bottom shambling past the street sign there? It was bright and chilly. Sinbad turned to reenter the house and found the window closing behind him. A pretty kettle of fish this was.

He was meant to fly, then.

He appraised the scene. A windy blue sky, jumbles of rooftops, pigeons. To his left the terrain rose vertically in stone higher than trees. That was the obvious place to take bearings. Sinbad ruffled his feathers and leapt into the breeze.

He had forgotten that in his youth certain muscles in his wings had been severed as a precaution against such escapades as this. Because the surgery was imperfect or because his vigor had tended to cancel its effects, Sinbad didn't stoop to his death, but flight would hardly be the word for his topsy-turvy gyrations. Too astonished to utter cries of alarm, he tumbled through the air across the street until more by chance than design he alighted on an ornamental ledge on the front of a house. He shut his eyes and then opened them. At the bottom of the street stood old Alex (yes, that was his unforgettable profile with vile stogie) gaping up at the very crest of rock Sinbad had meant to fly to. Otherwise no sign of life in the street. It could hardly have been less like a jungle, and it was cold. "Tsk, tsk," said Sinbad. He made for where the ledge turned into the crevice between its house and the adjacent one. Alex saw him and looked away. When he looked back, Sinbad had turned the corner.

Monday after five Julien Schumann tended his bookstore in the upper town by himself. When the last customer had gone he locked up and drove home. Many stores in the upper town were still open for Christmas shoppers but streets were empty in the lower town. Julien parked and walked toward his house on crackling new ice. At the corner, a voice clear as crystal laughed and said in Corneille's French, "Oh rage! Oh despair!

Inimical old age!" Julien listened. Vivid silence. Then in a voice not quite a scream, whose gender he couldn't determine, "Have I lived so long for this infamy?"

Julien approached old Pascale Mackenzie's house where the voice seemed to originate. He watched and listened in the dark freezing air. Julien was no more than two meters away when Pascale flung open her shutters. Each watched to see what the other would do next until the voice shrilled again, "Rage!" Pascale held up a hand—"Wait!"—and beckoned Julien through her house and out the back where a third time they heard the wild Corneille coming over the low wall from Catanese's dark greenhouse. Julien had to break the lock young Clusel had installed. Inside, Julien and Pascale found Alex Van Frank's missing parrot. Pascale went to telephone Alex. He and Anne arrived within minutes. Meanwhile Catanese reading in his bedroom had heard the commotion and come down expecting to find more vandalism in progress.

Sinbad hadn't known if he and Alex would ever be reunited. He was so glad to see the old geezer he flew straight at him, landed on his shoulder and held on for dear life, so tight his claws pierced the wool and cotton and went into Alex's flesh. Alex felt like clouting the dumb bird in the kisser but he kept gritting his teeth and grinning, and holding Anne close beside him while the flashbulbs went off.

Sinbad had lost 150 grams and he had bronchitis and fungal infections between his toes. Life in the crawl space under the greenhouse had been no honeymoon. The cold was the worst of it. Sinbad would have frozen solid without the radiator pipes under the floor, or had their insulation been better—whenever he could feel warmth coming through he pecked at it and a little more came through. He slept huddled against those places. There was a grated opening in the foundation wall that Catanese ought to have boarded up for the winter. Light and mice entered the crawl space there, but so did cold. Near the grate the ground froze and stayed frozen. Sometimes the most terrible wind came in and whistled around the pilings. Day after night after day after night, it got colder and colder until one night it grew acute because the radiator pipes were freezing. Huddled against the torn insulation Sinbad felt the temperature fall. He pressed closer for the warmth. There was less and less. Sinbad grew frantic and with the strength of desperation tore his way up through a weak place in the floor into the greenhouse. It was warm and he rested, but he soon realized that the temperature was falling here too. It was nightmarish. Beyond the glass walls and ceilings it was colder still. It was a horror show and Sinbad protested in the cries that brought Julien Schumann and Pascale Mackenzie to his rescue.

Sinbad ate mice in the crawl space, insects, spiders, vegetable matter off the pilings, bits of insulation. Mostly though he went hungry, especially earlier. Had he foreseen a tenth of the tribulation in store for him under the greenhouse he would have turned tail at first sight of it. The ledge he had half-flown, half-blown to from the Van Frank window took him around the corner back between houses. From the ledge he climbed a downspout to the rooftops and proceeded over them to the one with a view of the greenhouse.

In the beginning there was access to the crawl space from inside, and the door of the greenhouse had been ajar. Sinbad slipped in because it looked as if it contained a jungle. Inside was warm but dry, and the vegetation looked like a patch of jungle that had lost its flexibility and most of its color from swelling. Sinbad was exploring and had noticed a small opening in the floor and walked over for a closer look when he heard the door open wider and close. He thought perhaps it was the stranger who had evicted him—perhaps he hadn't yet done what it wanted. He hopped down through the opening onto cold earth. He listened to the tread he was to hear again and again. Catanese came into view above, an unhappy figure in black with slow movements that frightened Sinbad. It darkened the opening and then passed. Sinbad heard ominous little noises from time to time and then with a rumble the opening above closed. Then the footsteps, the greenhouse door opening and closing.

Several days passed during which Sinbad did everything he could to stave off terror. That was before he discovered the heat leaks in the insulation, nor had he yet learned what he could eat in the crawl space. He hadn't gone hungry a day in his life before and he was starving. For an eternity there were occasional noises above, unhurried footsteps, creaks. Sinbad couldn't have stood it another second when with a rumble the way into the greenhouse opened like an hallucination. Sinbad heard Catanese walk across overhead. He heard the greenhouse door open and close. He thought he heard Catanese walk away on snow, and a more distant door. He stuck his head through the hole. Nothing moved, least of all the succulents. Outside it was snowing. Sinbad scrambled up into the greenhouse. It was warm.

So it was that, to slake his delirious hunger and thirst, Sinbad proceeded to wreak the carnage that had disquieted Catanese. And as the man absorbed the shock and set about the salvage, there beneath his feet lay the culprit with diarrhea and toes insulted by sharp leaves, who saw his escape hatch close for the second and last time. Parrots are judgment-proof but were there a question of reparations Catanese's benefit would tell against his loss, for the cries that saved Sinbad also saved the plants. Neighbors helped restore the heat and celebrated the reunion of man and bird, recording it in photos, one of which appeared in the newspaper. Patrick Clusel, who took the photo, gave Alex an enlarged color print, which Alex framed and hung on his dining room wall. Sammy over in Lévis asked why he didn't make a painting of it. What the hell, Alex said, photography is an art now. I read it in a magazine.

In the close-up Anne's face is tightened. She almost smiles, her eyes already scouting for the next disaster. Alex looks ready to take even the pope under his free arm. He grins for Spinoza and Venus, he beams with exoneration. Between them you see blue, green, and yellow Sinbad. A wing touches Alex's cheek. The bird has turned his head at right angles to his breast, to bill the crown of Alex's head. His black eye is the brightest in the picture.

Soon the mystery of how Sinbad came to be in the greenhouse ceased to concern anyone. Alex and Anne supposed that one of them had left the cage unlocked, and that the parrot had somehow found his way out of the house and to the greenhouse on his own, as could perfectly well have happened.

It seemed likely that Alex would die before Anne and Sinbad, probably during the next decade, and his body be reduced to ash. The separatist sentiment in Québec would subside, and Anne be grateful it hadn't happened earlier. And old Sinbad would take food from her hand and speak in her voice, and Catanese sell the house in the upper town he by then never used, and the ferry ply the river as before.

Saint Silvère's Head

The passenger boat from Marseille to Tunis leaves in the early afternoon and takes twenty-four hours to cross the Mediterranean. You may try to sleep out the bumpy night in a cabin bed or sit frugally in the lounge with destitute Arabs—whichever, your spirits rise around noon and you think Africa itself must be minutes away when you pass the first landfall, the island of La Galite (Jeziret Jalita). In fact you still have two good hours to go, and the trip would be even longer were you traveling between the island and Bizerte or Tunis in one of the smaller slower fishing boats that provide the only access to La Galite, now as in the thirties when Saint Silvère lost his head.

La Galite is an irregular crescent some seven kilometers long and three wide at its widest, with a good natural harbor. Several far smaller islands lie within sight. Les Chiens aren't much more than a pair of barnacled rocks, the lonely lighthouse stands atop Le Galiton, and finally there is La Fauchelle, with its black rabbits.

The Galitois of fifty years ago and their ancestors had come to the island from coastal cities and towns in Italy, Tunisia, and France. They spoke a kind of French Neapolitan with many Arabic words and phrases. The men fished the surrounding waters for *langouste* and sold their catch in the mainland harbors, where they and their families used the money for a few luxuries—a magazine, a fancy rooster—and what few necessities they were unable to provide for themselves. For they were very nearly self-sufficient. With the *langouste* they took fish and squid from the sea, and around the island's rocky shore they gathered limpets, urchins, octopus and sometimes gull eggs. They had olive and fruit trees, raised many vegetables and kept chickens, sheep, goats, and pigs, and made their own wine, cheese, bread, and sausage and their own clothes and shoes.

Mariadjire, called the Greek because you couldn't understand her, had the little grocery near the water and Conchette had the one on the hill. But even these, the only commercial establishments besides the tiny bar at the harbor, were merely rooms in the white flat-roofed cottages. No one had electric lights or telephones. Islanders drew fresh water from wells, trying not to disturb the eel that lived in one, and for their laundry they used rain water and ashes. A few families had outhouse sheds but for most there was simply a latrine in a clearing in the bamboo some distance from the house.

Conchette of the upper grocery, by the way, had the island's only cow, whose good milk she sold at a fair price or drank herself. Years later in the south of France this same Conchette disgraced herself and her family with milk. She had developed a habit of stealing a bottle before dawn from one of the crates left by the dairy truck in front of the neighborhood grocery, and the owners took a flashbulb picture of her in the act.

Had such a thing happened before Conchette left La Galite, she would surely have been given a name to commemorate it. Children as they grew up learned two names for many of the adults. Jacomine the Tripod and Elise the Viper had three daughters, Eliane the Moray-Eel-in-a-Nun's-Habit, Rosette Ear-to-the-Ground, and Ninette the Cheese Grater because of her complexion. And there were stories and stories—

how one Sunday afternoon in the Café Riche in Bizerte a rat ran across the dance floor and bit Crazy Djoulina's shoe, how skinny Achilles the Strong saw a ghost near the lighthouse.

People called Lucia Matzel by the bland name of Zia (Aunt) Lucia. At the time of this story she was around fifty, a small lively widow with bright green eyes and a few long gray whiskers on her chin. She lived with her son, Silvère, who was barely twenty and didn't have a nickname yet. His father had been killed in an accident with the *langouste* trap lines after six months of marriage, before Silvère's birth. Lucia had grieved and stayed in mourning some longer than decorum required, and then she had looked about for another husband for a while until, finding none, she had reconciled herself to being Zia Lucia in the houses of her sisters and brothers and their families, and raising Silvère herself with their help.

Silvère at twenty had become one of the island's most eligible bachelors, cheerful and steady, handsome and a good sailor and fisherman. Some islanders opined that Zia Lucia would be a burden to whatever wife he might take, the love between mother and son was so strong. Otherwise the Galitois, who weren't at all slow to find fault, had mostly good to say about these two.

One morning around nine, when the large and small boats had been out several hours and were all a good distance from port, the sky darkened precipitously and a storm of unusual violence blew in out of the northwest and lasted until late afternoon, with gale winds and waves high enough to capsize any of the unlucky fleet. No island woman was more fearful than Zia Lucia, for that day Silvère had gone out in one of the smallest boats alone except for old Toto, who was a good sailor but slow and weak. More than Silvère's father had died at sea, and hardly a man was without injuries. Near the top of the ridge Zia Lucia at her parlor window looked out over Papa Nioque's roof (which served her as a terrace for drying figs and cod) down into the harbor where by noon only five boats had struggled in to dock, none of them her son's.

Half an hour later she saw Silvère's boat coasting in past Le Galiton. She had prayed for his safety to the Virgin and Saint Lucia, and especially to Saint Silvère, kneeling in front of the wooden effigy that stood under a bell jar on a stand beside her hearth, clothed in silk pope's robes and crowned with the orange blossoms she had worn as a bride. Now she went out onto her terrace to wave a scarf in the wind to welcome Silvère. Others from their terraces and windows and doorways saw the scarf go to Zia Lucia's mouth as the ship came nearer and she saw that it wasn't Silvère's at all, but Hassen's which also happened to have a red prow.

By two the sky had cleared some and the wind wasn't quite so fierce. Three boats that had been fishing together in the west filed in, one with a sheared mast. By then Zia Lucia had learned that Toto and Silvère had last been seen making for La Galite in midmorning. By three theirs was one of two boats missing. Zia Lucia lifted the heavy bell jar off Saint Silvère and laid aside the dry coronet. She turned the saint around, picked him up and ran out to the edge of her terrace, holding Saint Silvère straight out toward the sea, for him to use all his power to bring back his namesake.

Galitois dogs ate well enough, and had children to play with and rabbits to chase into the brush, but from adult islanders they might receive a solid kick, delivered in Arab disdain and amiable southern European contempt, as easily as a good hustling of the fur over their shoulders. Those who didn't bear their lot with equanimity became fish bait but some, like rangy old brown-and-white Reziel, whose mistress lived in the lane above Zia Lucia's, might engage in wary mischief now and then. And a storm excited and frightened the dogs more than other island animals.

Old Reziel was loping by when Zia Lucia brought out

Saint Silvère. He paused and perked up his ears. Zia Lucia prayed aloud for her son's safety. Then by some mischance the saint's head tumbled from his shoulders. Zia Lucia's eyes widened as the head rolled away from her feet across the terrace in the wind. Old Reziel watched too and then with a bound he picked the saint's head up in his mouth and ran.

Appalled, Zia Lucia watched Reziel stop and turn halfway back toward her so that he could watch without seeming to, like a puppy at play, rump in the air and elbows on the cobbles. Saint Silvère's pious whitened resignation to the sixth-century turns of fortune that would result in his martyrdom—as well as the latest affronts of being several meters from his body and framed in teeth and loose jowls—shone sideways, the normally heavenward gaze now directed over the rooftops to the wild sea. Zia Lucia's neighbors who had seen her carry out the icon watched in a kind of silence that spread under the howl of the wind, the event was so unpropitious.

"Filthy beast!" Zia Lucia rushed forward waving the headless saint as if she intended to club Reziel with it. He, sensing the gravity of his misdeed, dropped his prize and scooted under a fence. Zia Lucia might have had the head then if she'd been faster, but it began to move over the cobbles along the path that wound between fields and garden plots and houses down to the harbor. The head slowed as it rolled through a depression and up a mild incline, where it seemed to pause. Gasping "Aie! Aie!," Zia Lucia tried to corner it with her foot. Instead she tipped it over, and it bounced three times down a ten-step stair and continued on its way. At the top Zia Lucia, too winded to run more, crossed herself as if the untoward omen were the actual death of her son. The head caromed off Maria Radze's garden wall and skittered across the path at an angle into the corner formed by the walls of Lucrèce Darco's house and her dead father's empty one, where it stopped. Fifteen years later, when Habib Bourguiba was confined for a time on the island he lived in Lucrèce Darco's father's house.

A neighbor recalled hearing of Saint Silvère's more drastic confinement on an island in the Ligurian, and said that Zia Lucia's effigy must have foreseen Bourguiba's coming.

The wind was yowling. Zia Lucia, her rope-soled canvas shoes flapping, Saint Silvère's chasuble and skirts billowing from under her arm, came down fast as she could and retrieved the head, which she replaced and then there where she stood once more pointed the intact icon toward the black harbor. She gave it a gentle but entirely firm shake, as though it were a recalcitrant child. Almost horizontal, a boat slipped in out of the rain into the harbor's lee where it righted itself enough for islanders to see it was Kagaliose's. A shout went up from his house and from others on the hillside. Zia Lucia crossed herself once more since Kagaliose's safety seemed a possible omen that Silvère and Toto would shortly come limping in to port themselves. She climbed back up to her house.

Dusk was falling now, and it seemed to happen more slowly than usual for simultaneously the sky was clearing as the storm made its way east past Tunis and Carthage and south, passing well above Djerba la Douce and dissipating as it went until it must have made landfall in Libya and died in the sands. On La Galite lanterns and lamps were being lighted in houses and down at the harbor. Galitois visited neighbors to hear news of damage the wind might have done on the island, and of what had happened at sea. From house to house went the story of Lucia, old Reziel and Saint Silvère's head. Each time the story was told anew, a cautious alertness would come over the room, and speaker and audience would search one another's eyes for amusement, as they crossed themselves or laid hands over hearts. Whenever some glimmer threatened to break through the solemnity, they would think of Zia Lucia waiting alone and afraid for her son.

Before night fell, before it was too dark for the dash from the shoal beyond Les Chiens where he had spent the worst of the storm at anchor, Silvère brought his boat home. As he and old Toto came ashore, they learned that this storm had taken no friend's life. Toto set out on the path that led around a hill to the house consisting of a cave with a door and windows built over its entrance where he lived with his brother. Silvère headed up the path to his mother's, and word of his arrival preceded him. Along the way fellow sailors and their families and other islanders stepped out of their houses to clap him on the shoulders and joke, and Zia Lucia stood in front of her house waving and brushing some tears from under her eyes until her son stepped onto the terrace with her and she could put her arms around him. She didn't mind in the least that already the story of Saint Silvère's head was being retold, this time with the laughter that had been withheld before. She herself would laugh as much as they did. Today around the Mediterranean and elsewhere people who know that Zia Lucia must have died, and who remember her dimly if at all, still sometimes tell the story. It continues to give pleasure, in the safety of its time.

As told by Yves Orvoën

THINKING MACHINES

In some irrecoverable case study of two decades ago, a schizophrenic maintained that his apparently ramshackle artifacts of string, wire, and scraps of wood or metal were machines. He maintained that they made his thought possible, or even produced it.

Attention, Shoppers

If some of you've failed to provision for the upcoming Folly Day weekend, you'll find the third-floor staff already grinning. On your way there, do stop by the shelter for a pedicure, you'll like it more than you thought you would. While you're husking, why not try your luck with our yum-yum draw? Anybody might win, you might, it's possible, hurry right over.

Taking a look at amenities, we have them in spades if you will, every known brand, four floors down in the skank zone, many still under wraps. You'll want to give yourselves more than ample time for browsing there! And speaking of stocking up, don't forget to let us show you the new lizard grab bags, you'll want one in each of several depths. Heads up, Gucci bear fans, specials yet remain. Enjoy.

"Enjoy" takes me back to an earlier time, simpler, before Prince and Aporia even, back before the twelfth of never, when products were products if you know what I mean, when hype was hype if you follow. Remember vinyl? Who doesn't sometimes hanker after this or that trace of a time when we all cottoned to person-effects, consequences, terror (ha-ha), grits, and shucks. So get this: you want, you got. Why wait? No need to deny yourselves a minute longer. Just make tracks and check out our full assortment of retrofits. Remember mainframes? Remember Princess Vanna? Remember what fun a good laugh was, when all you had to do was make the moves and noises?

Speaking of which, when the opportunity arises all of you will want to belly up to the resumption tables out at the east end of aisle 387. You'll like what you see there, no question about that. Of course supplies are limited, so pop on over when you see your way clear.

Shoppers with a yen for the concrete can snap up some hot simulacra after changing currency. This week we phase in gridirons, griddlecakes, gippers, and gridlocks, and down the road a ways we see polecats coming on strong. Don't be caught napping, consumers! Fork over, fork on and on, you'll like it more than you thought you could. You'll need it, everybody needs purchasing power, everybody wants to plunk something down somewhere, possessions quickly pay for themselves in gabble, shoppers.

Nothing could be more gratifying than a sparkling new agenda for the holidays. You'll find them on the east buffalo wing mezzanine, trot over, we have them from half a sec, in every length—and the longer the agenda the bigger the bargain, as you have every right to expect with us.

Looking for a new pair of Big Bird shoes? You'll find them tucked between printouts and sclerotics, all lined up in your own personal sizes on the footwear shelves behind the fresh compassion display. Hightail it, aficionados. Nothing warms the cockles more than three or four new pairs, as I myself well know when I recall my first pair winking at me from under the bushy boughs when I was a mere sixteen, a mere knot on a log if I may, a good five decades ago anyway. Shoppers, when I first slid my toots into those beauts and slid across the permaseal I felt more serene than Goethe ice-skating in the old picture. They stood me in good stead and so have their successors. In later years, when spouse Icterine has secreted me a new pair to peek through the icicles, it was never exactly because their predecessors had worn thin, and not really because the dogs had expanded either. No, it was more because of the inevitable dispersal and dilution—disappearance, even—of valuable novelty. Come to think, here in the cubicle at this very moment when I wiggle the piggies I can detect that telltale pedal itch for the good old unfamiliar. How about you? Creeping up the gams? Rush to footwear, the newest Big Birds wait there for the pawing, and you'll find heaps of kneepads too, not to mention footpads and earplugs.

Browsers, don't bark the wrong tree if you don't have to, or rather want to: at or near each interface you'll probably find obedient programs recapping every scene, sphere of influence, and doodad. Take pine siskins and their range. Take five piney-wood allusive Tonto substitutes home with you tonight if you have room behind the eightball, you'll enjoy them every time they remind you. Take a powder and take Sis skiing in one of our alpine vac packs. In the train you'll bemuse yourselves with one of the new domino theories from Barker Brothers. You'll have loads of fun visiting lost places and miserable places, and the action-packed ten-day weekend includes an audience with the Tooth Fairy, plus more hot potatoes than you can shake a stick at, all already carefully jacketed for your convenience in handling. Moony for something farther afield? At the junket modules atop any handy eatery you can land conceptual space galore in this or that satellite, equipped for the blast of a lifetime.

A little gaggle of words about the noise piping through you this hour from central sporting. If it has a whiff of familiarity, Muzak fans, here's why: it's dribbles and backboard vibes carefully rerouted and deferred by wizardry. Should you hanker after some for private consumption, nothing could be easier. You'll want to accessorize it with a corps of the trial balloons you see dancing over many of your heads. Just imagine the pride of ownership.

Remember, shoppers, it's always a treat to schlep back for a turn in your new Big Birds at the ballroom compound, where this hour we're screening recolorized video clips of an earlier generation slam dunking. Cheap at any price, so give yourself a break even if you don't deserve it, you'll like it more than anything else while you do it. Not to worry if the two-step doesn't quite come naturally—we have Bronislava and Vaslav, Arthur and Catherine, Ginger and Fred, and other reconstituted hoofers for instruction and taxiing. These magic moments convert easily into small talk.

Try food and edibles for important confections now surfacing in Double Dutch, our Flavor of the Moment, and while there do waylay one of our Staff of Life circulating with encouraging looks and trays of bouchées—I personally never find myself able to resist the hegemonies. In the darkroom you'll distinguish freeze-dried slabs of dark meat locked in for your delectation. Take-out munchies are comestible in-shop of course. Pack several rustler specials away in the duffle, or eat and run the next time you pass an access slit. You can easily locate them by following the trails of crumbs and packaging.

As far as room is concerned, you'll find every sort, both collapsed and inflated displayed where available. Choose among arcana to rent or lease, or own your own under a practically endless array of mortgage configurations, as well as all the latest deeds. Plunk it down, shoppers: capitalized deconstruction of mobile homelands has been roaring as you know, and in a marketer's market the name of the game is plunk. Nothing's more fun than moving, and our models come fully equipped with mats and racks, vistas and disposals, and throttles and easements, all with the highest recognition value for your credit. Particular affect treatments include façades gently problematized with effigies of bare ruined acquirers.

Go to it, shoppers. Avid for one another? Flock over to one of the conduits to our revolving registry, where you'll find every arrangement available, from perpetual possession on out. Those of you currently espousing may or may not choose continuation. Whatever your choice, we can make you like it better, so don't wait, we're all shysters and druthers under the skin. Maybe I'm corny, but I can't help mentioning that my own Icterine and I picked each other out here ourselves, back when the registry had a lacy effect with twittering lights, any number of years ago.

Not to suggest anything in particular, by the way. Permanence is a function of impermanence, and bliss is where you choose to buy it, to echo one of our framed signifiers. You'll find them in the upper left hemisphere. And nearby, a pittance gives you your interlude with the signifieds in their distinctive flight, alternately bunching up and then dispersing in undulations, like a sky full of shoppers. Finally, before we switch on the next brownout, do make a mental note of the bargain reassurance now dwindling in our nether region. Crawl fast, it won't wait, and better luck next time if it's already gone.

For Nineteen Sixty-eight

1

Such a slipshod slapdash forest of a jungle I'd never seen or imagined or even wanted to—it was partly that it was green and dull gray and partly that it was so hot and wet I'd long ago doffed my pack and my shirt and partly that with every step I took more and more leaves and grass clung to my trousers—I'd begun to look like a shaggy-legged satyr—and also that it was dead quiet, there were simply no animals to be heard: it reminded me of a bad photograph: things seemed a little greasy, a little slick, like those lights that nag underneath the eyeballs, those almost-colorless ones, it reminded me of that French phrase *comme ci, comme ça,* a little sinister but more just deadening, just tiresome, the vines I held to pull myself along, even they were almost colorless or changed their little colors and could have gone any which way, I could hardly bear to think about it, "ugh" was the only word for it or "whew," it wasn't particularly sunny but it was hot, and sometimes the vines fell or came apart in my hands and there wasn't a flower to be seen, it all looked cheap and washed-up and passed-over like Florida or Vietnam or what have you, I half-expected the vines to be neon signs with their letters burned out, I remember I said to myself it was as much a time as a place, a welter of eventless conditions, I said there were none of those difficulties that stand up to be counted but only the kind that glimmer and persist, a low flux of a rundown maze like a fever with momentary outlines glassily precise but inconstant, there were no landmarks, my age was age as much as strength and yet the fatigued wonder was more of my mind than my body, it reminded me of the statues in Rome when Dorothea Brooke wandered among them, partly because there was no passion and partly because there was a kind of blind, shifty clarity, and then the fulsome air, and the decay that made me wonder if my eyes themselves had decayed or something similar—I could see the unclean magic of words like *et cetera,* the only sound was my struggle, and I thought of any number of emotions but they all seemed inappropriate, with the mud and rubbish hanging to my legs, the vines against my shoulders, here and there the wrong light, it reminded me of mental illness and shell shock, as if my thoughts were slowing down or stopping, the whole thing was like dirty neon somehow, the whole thing was like every step I took, it was like the preternatural vividness of a dead language, shopping lists in a dead language, I trudged on.

2

I broke through into the edge of a large clearing, in the middle of which I saw rambling flimsy structures like barracks built of unpainted wood and bamboo, some with thatched roofs. There were no shadows because, as I now saw, the sky was overcast with a brilliant gray haze. The soil I stepped onto was poor and sandy and littered with straw and scraps of paper and other refuse. It reminded me of an abandoned fairground. Everything seemed straw-colored. I must have simply stood there without moving for a long time, breathing. There was a soft persistent sound like the whine of a TV set. I saw that there were bits of food on the ground, and then here and there about the compound—I called it that in my mind—I saw a number of men sitting and lying on the ground. Unshaven and sun-browned, clothed in little more than faded shorts or loincloths, they made me think of Robinson Crusoe, except that they were inactive and unobservant. The few that noticed me showed no sign of interest. It occurred to me that they seemed drugged—perhaps by the warmth or the clear hazy light, or even the soft whine. They were thin but not emaciated. I sat down and took off my boots, and then stood and walked into the clearing.

A young woman wearing khaki shorts and a halter came forward from among the buildings. Her body was supple and beautiful, her step light. What struck me most forcibly was the color of her skin: glossy as though oiled, a hard rich copper with purple and orange surface lights. It made a taste like blood come into my mouth. It was seductive but flat and powerful, like the bright skin of a snake. She reminded me of an Arab or Israeli soldier. On her arms and shoulders and the rise of her breasts there was what I took to be pollen until I realized that it was dry fine dust. She was—how shall I say it—she was unconcerned. She might as well have been naked. She was a Circe for my time, that was it. The clearing was a compound. I was in a kind of concentration camp. She might as well have carried a machine gun.

I don't know whether I mounted her—that was the only word for it—immediately or not. It was clear that I should do so often and mechanically. The next thing I remember is this: she gave me a tour of the buildings where I would be quartered.

They were, as I have said, low and barrackslike and flimsy; they surrounded a number of interior courts open to the sky. There were no single rooms, only narrow meandering corridors. As we walked through them she indicated with a cursory gesture the sleeping accommodations: rattan mats scattered about the floors, a few cots, a hammock, here and there banks of shelves attached to a wall. Many of the men lay inside—we had to step over several as we made our way along—but the place was far from crowded. We paused long enough for one of the men to have his pleasure of her, and then proceeded.

Probably because of the fine sand the buildings stood on, they seemed strangely clean, like things in the desert or on the seashore. The matter still clinging to my legs had dried and lightened. I felt the sort of euphoria that comes at the end of long fatigue and sleeplessness. I watched the woman's waist as she walked in front of me. When she spoke she hardly deigned to glance at me. She was mine as entirely as she was the rest of the men's, and we were hers. There was something that had been in my mind and it was gone and I could not imagine what it had been. I listened to the thin whine and the soft footfalls of our naked feet. When any of the men glanced at me, there was nothing at all in his clear eyes.

Finally, we came out again into the compound that surrounded the buildings. As I could see, the brilliant sky was a gray very slight blacker than it had been before. The two of us stood there together side by side for a long time.

I noticed that the stockade was bounded with a high woven bamboo-and-grass wall, above which I could see the tops of palms and other trees and the tangle of vines. I realized that each detail of this vista, and of everything else in the enclosure, would become unspeakably familiar to me, more familiar than my own body, than my own face, which I was already beginning to forget. Most familiar of all would be the woman beside me, who had locked herself in my attention with her negligence and her coppery eyes. I stood breathing. There seemed a peculiar right in all the wrong. I had no sense of direction and I hardly cared. I had a sort of equilibrium, at least I had that.

3

But things did not come entirely to a halt: as I stood there gazing over the littered sand I noticed a disturbance at the edge of the compound. I saw that there was a place where the wall had been pushed down or had simply dropped inward so that it lay flat on the ground. And there I saw a cluster of women, not like the woman in the camp, but pale and turbulent with their colored rags. They seemed to have just discovered the opening in the fence, and to be hesitating between attack and retreat. They reminded me of animals thronging to the edges of a circle of firelight. They pushed one another and chattered and stared. Their clothes were in rags and they seemed to be carrying primitive weapons, blowguns perhaps, bows or spears or even stones. They were brave and frightened. What shook me was the realization that they with their pale and soft skin and their savagery might have represented rescue for me and the other men, a primitive and turbulent rescue crowded there in the opening of the fence. I would have beckoned to them or laughed aloud.

I could see that it was very slightly darker. Perhaps the soft whine was deepening toward a noise like thunder very far away or the whisper of an airplane. Perhaps the air had cooled by one or two degrees. I looked before me and I saw a band of women crouched like a pitiful war party in the opening of the stockade, wearing their courage like gaudy rags. It was intolerable. In my heart I begged them to rush into the compound. I looked at their dark eyes and their tender white skin. They were shaking their weapons and chattering ominously there in the opening of the stockade.

4

Many things are hard to remember and harder to understand, especially the ones that surround and hold the others. A glove can enclose a hand and at the same time, or even if it's empty, hold an orange in its palm. But one time stands out clearly from the others. It was late at night and I had finished the chores that then filled up most of my waking hours. A few hours before, I had spoken with a certain person about a matter of some importance; we had reached no decision, and had arranged to talk again soon. Now I wandered out onto my porch or patio under the open sky to think. The weather was typical of that part of the country and that season; there was a little wind.

I sat down and smoked a cigarette or two at my leisure. The stars were very bright and clear. They made me think of silent machine-gun fire scattered above me. Nearby was a sound like a soft footfall. I watched the sky for a long time until like a jungle my difficulties grew up around me again, demanding attention, which I gave—resignedly, and with good humor. At length I put out my last cigarette and returned to the house. I remember that before I went to sleep I looked out my window, and saw the trees begin to shake under the bright sky.

Duckwalking

I was down in the mouth, Martha was upstairs with the kids, in his first tube series Rick Montalban was playing a DA—a welcome switch from the detective cycle according to Hearst Motion Picture Editor Dorothy Manners (HMPEDM). I'd had flak that day from the boss about some quantification, it was quite a flap and I was feeling like chucking it. Being a 'puter programmer (PP), I knew I wouldn't lack for work. I'd popped a Quaalude and Rick was wrapping up a smack baron when down the stairs comes Martha doing it. I said, "Oh really?" She gave me a Bronx cheer through the banister rails.

We'd talked about it but I hadn't expected her to start just like that. I think she'd been practicing in secret 'cause she got down the stairs okay. She kicked off her mukluks and came over and stood with her elbow on the coffee table. A laxative ad, a Melmac ad, some gag-rule claptrap on the news before she looks away from the screen. "Doc Purdy says forget bursitis."

"Purdy's no doc, he's . . ."

Martha interrupted, "I've made up my mind, Bill, and I'm not backing out. Noon news showed Jackie doing it at a function. If you want to look like a cracker, that's your problem." They were showing Iraqi quake damage footage before back to Rick, who was in hot water. Catherine Spaak, a skyjacker, had winged him. Martha said, "It's easier than I thought though."

"You fracture me. Five'll getcha ten you don't make it through the weekend." That was a Friday.

That weekend we backpacked with Arch and Tiffany Drake. Arch was a PP too, freelancing at the time. We'd talked about leaving kids home but decided not to. Bill Jr. was fifteen and Martha Jr.'d've been eleven, with Arch and Tiff's in the same bracket. Ours had tried it now and again around the house, and Martha Jr. could already roller-skate doing it. Saturday morning when we took stuff out to the car, they and their mother were all doing it. They all stayed down most of that weekend and from then on, except that for half a year Martha Jr. might pop up for a laugh.

Arch and Tiff tooted and waved (T&W): "Let's book." I backed out and followed them to the wilderness area parking lot. The kids didn't stop yakking. They were playing tic-tac-toe in the back and when one won he or she would give the other a good thwack. I was too sicky-poo about employment snafus to mind. Arch parked his Wankel Mach II smack-dab at the end of the lot and when he and Tiff stepped down out I saw that they were doing it. Their kids were too.

The Joy of Cacking, the conglom that owned the one I'd been PPing for for a couple of years, had a knack for diversification. They'd just bought into Cunard, and office platitude had it the next step was to work some Peking action as a decoy to wangle tax shrinkage. That would draw ack-ack, but J of C had a gaggle of tricks up its sleeve and its future looked anything but lackadaisical. It was playing glitz ball, so what was racking my brains that Saturday was all I stood to lose or gain moving to a new conglom or freelancing like Arch. Arch and I'd been chums years and so had Tiff and Martha. Arch and Tiff are Quakers but you wouldn't want to meet a wackier couple, so I aimed to bend Arch's ear about my job sometime during the weekend.

All the rucksacks but mine dragged, and seeing how slow the going up the trail was didn't make me eager to get down. On the other hand they all chatted like mad and I kept having to bend over to follow. We hit the site about two and pitched camp. After a macaroon snack the kids waddled off to gather kindling, the girls were chewing the cud about a boutique and Arch and I broke out a six-pack and axes and split a few logs. Handling the axe down there was easier for him than I'd expected. Then we sat on the woodpile and rapped.

"What's eating you, Bill? You look like you want to duke it out with somebody." I got worked up letting off steam about the job but Arch didn't crack a smile. He said, "Listen, Mac, that's hooey. I'd hang tight in your place. This rickrack with the boss'll blow over. You and Martha should invite him and Khakeline bowling." He said J of C's quark angle looked good and in fact he himself planned to hook up on a permanent basis since freelancing was getting too flaky too quick. The kids were moving back into the clearing over by the douches. Martha Jr. missed a softball from Arch Jr. that would've beaned me if I hadn't bobbed my head down in time. Arch grinned, "Dangerous up there, Bill," as he scooted off his log and started toward the fire. I rose to follow and old Arch looked up and said, "Why not give it a try?"

It was dusk, and I remember the crackling of the campfire as I thought, "Why not?" And I remember how the trees wagged as I squatted. Arch and I ambled over to the fire where the wives were cooking a lip-smacking wokload of sprouts. "I knew you were up to it," Martha cooed, and she planted a peck on my kisser. I stayed down the rest of that weekend, kayaking through quagmires and brackish shallows, nearly losing tackle to a bull mackerel I finally landed, relaxing at Tiff's after-lunch songfest cacophony, I stayed down. It sure was good to take a gander right or left and ogle smirks instead of empty air.

That was, oh, seven or eight years ago, when to lots like

me duckwalking (DW) looked weak on staying power and thin on consequence. Little did we know. To backtrack, I had first heard of it a year or so before on a wrap-up of what older young adults had been into. One segment dealt with a Texas air force base brouhaha where a Big Mac maître d' who'd channeled incoming customers flat south of a DWing waitress got hooted by a WAC claque. I remember I said, "Those squirts." Martha said yes, but she'd scanned a Sunday supplement piece a while back about it that made it sound fun. Later you heard about it more frequently and then somebody said he'd seen a gentleman doing it here in town, over on Thirty-third near the shellac factory. The exact reason why it eventuated is still in question, but discos were one of the places it seemed to catch on first. The Cow-cow Mooie, the Wigwag, and the Macaque were only three of the steps it hatched. *TV Guide* ran a New Year's spread about it with a snap of that month's Neilsen pinup doing it with the Whackers' quarterback at New York's Bimbo's overlooking Central Park. Videoland in fact was a pacesetter. A daytime game show anchorlady sometimes came on doing it, and then on a novelty series about a paramedic and his favorite Tommy gun the whole cast did it. Flicks caught on and novelizations followed fast on their heels.

In the sports world the change raised a few hackles. Most squawks centered on the gridiron 'cause it slowed the game so much. But that was true of all the running sports, and rule changes must've had umps cracking books even when they went potty. Fans groused but there was no denying that tactics, especially blocking and tackling, were easier to qualitate. Backboards got lowered for hoopsters; batters' and pitchers' styles underwent more far-reaching changes than catchers'. With these like other team sports the field of play naturally shrank so playtime could approximate foregoing commitments to duration length. Ditto for track, double-dog ditto for broad and high jump. The underhand disappeared from tennis, but in swimming the breast- and backstroke needed only slight kick modifications. Billiards survived intact on a lowered table, and jockeys required minimal stirrup-strap hitches.

The presidential lackey squad gave out he personally affirmed DW's gassiness for some months until after one State of the Union Gossipcast (SUG) he slid off the official banquette and didn't stand but instead did it off the stage. Some hacks penned quasi-clucks, others marked it up to sprightly daffiness. The short podium at his next confab told us we were eyeballing the beginning of an era. Armed forces were quick to follow suit. I recall some bivouacked Cossacks surviving a surprise attack with no more than dented helmets.

Of course it infused new fuel into the economy. Take slacks: looser knees cried out for alterations in factory process-components that themselves had to be designed and produced in other factories. Ripples big as tidal waves raced every which way.

My own life has taken several new tacks. For a month after that memorable weekend I sometimes thought of standing back up, but I stayed down and my relations with Martha and the kids waxed smoother pronto. One evening as we gathered on our tatamis around the din-din table Bill Jr. turned to me and cackled, "Pap, hunkering here with you and the big M and Sis-face makes me sure I'm the luckiest little pecker alive." My ticker got gooey.

As far as old Martha and me are concerned, that weekend beside the picnic table we started to re-relate (RR) and as the new stance grew on us we found ourselves chitchatting more. The mechanics of sex haven't had to change too much of course, and the actual act gets done at least as often as before duckwalking (BD). At the drop of a hat she'll say, "Drag those knackers over here, Bill"—she's still in bed, it's Sunday, I've showered and before I even dry my back we're banging. We sleep streetcar. Sometimes in the beginning I'd stretch the gams in bed but now the fronts of my knees nuzzle the backs of hers. She's still stacked. The other day we were readying to step next door for drinkypoos and an Also Sprach tape. Old Martha had on a black Shantung poly mini and platform flippers. The placket wobbled like a raccoon tail and I went gaga all over again when she sidled over for a buss.

Like everybody we enjoyed a spate of redecorating in the beginning. We were in a semidetached bungalow in hock up to our necks so we made do with ladders and step-ups, our old gimcrack furniture, lowered macramé and spice racks and shorter wastebaskets. Now we're in the condo with all new chopped Louis XIV and a recessed waterbed. Martha's acquired some slick bric-a-brac at the Knicknack Shack down the block. A set of Now Faces in Composition Matter Plaques (NFCMP) tops the period baseboard.

Bosso got kicked upstairs soon after my little contretemps and with the new helmsman things have been cricket. Work's the same, but better. Puters' capacities explode monthly simultaneous to monthly hardware shrinkages, and programming's several magnitude notches above prior, but office routine's distinctly similar. So wall urinals have become straddle troughs, so what: everybody still wears baseball caps, gagsters stock whoopee cushions, and the Muzak's never run dry.

As to social life. The fam and I get off on floor tubefests with the neighbors now and again, as I've hopefully specified. Roller-rink Saturday matinees are a hoot, especially when we tap a keg. Golf is always golf even with lateral swings, and the Cheer Club plays nine when it's not hawking loquat pie and sausage for the subteen skateoramas. Bill Jr. and Martha Jr. have Trans Ams with glass packs. He plays wah-wah in the marching band and shortstop in the summer. She majorettes—her squad's the Whirlybirds. They both have part-time jobs and heartthrobs.

J of C's had more than its share of the DW prosperity. Somebody must've had an inside line 'cause just at the start, when most congloms had kissed off construction for a cash-flow bottleneck cork, and starts were scarcer than hen's teeth, J of C shifted its diversification exactly that way. As DW became a *fait accompli,* other gloms moved in for some pie too. Horizontal bisection of existing units was the rule, though some spaces accommodated tri- and hypertrisection, and none of the new plexes and rises has ceilings above four feet. Housing's had megabucks for a demidecade now and J of C's led the pack so I have plenty to crow about. True, some Jack or other over cocktails occasionally gets nostalgic about the upright posture we abandoned. But I say, after all, was it really ever more than a posture?

TRUE ROMANCES

The truth will make you free.

John 8:32

The romance is nearest of all literary forms to the wish-fulfilment dream . . . no matter how great a change may take place in society, romance will turn up again, as hungry as ever, looking for new hopes and desires to feed on.

Northrop Frye, *Anatomy of Criticism*, 1957

West Baltimore

"Say a prayer for me." Eight-thirty, half-toothless fat Margaret on the hot sidewalk, dark Italian lunes under sharp eyes, white hair in a shingle. "I don't go to church (why should I lie?) except for the lunches. The nun's from the south, I love her accent, she's nice." West Baltimore and Margaret born ten blocks from here over a grocery her parents ran, ten blocks and sixty-two years.

"But say a prayer for me anyway, Larry. My landlady said she's sold the house. Drove up yesterday in her big car. I told her I didn't know about the Sadanas—you know, the family from India that lives on the second floor. I said I didn't know about them or about Punky and his ma on the third floor—you know Punky, Larry. His ma don't get out. I said I didn't know about them either but me, I understood I could stay a year, so I said I aimed to stay for the seven months I got coming. I pay my rent. You want to be my lawyer?" Larry smiles, in a hurry to get to his summer-school law class. Eight-thirty, sidewalk already hot. "I been up since five, I always wake up early."

Marg's Tippy always wakes up first and waits for Margaret to, like this morning, five, just light. Marg puts on her housecoat and slippers and goes back through the kitchen to let

Tippy out in the yard. Tippy does her business down next the garbage cans and then comes back to be let in. Likes it in the house better, some dogs are like that.

"Fred here's Tippy's friend." He was a stray, pitiful when Marg started giving him a piece of bread now and then. "He's big but he's nice. Two or three times a day he comes around to say hello to me and Tippy." Marg doesn't have the teeth for a real ef. *Fred* in her mouth is a blurred *Pred.*

"Ever hear of a praying cat? Man up the street had one. Every morning it'd jump up on the chiffonier in front of the crucifix and cross its paws and close its eyes and pray. Lucy saw it, you know Lucy up the street."

Marg's been up since five. Fed Tippy, ate a piece of bread and drank a cup of tea looking at the TV and trying not to think about the landlady. The air wasn't real hot yet. Then she got her pail and brush and went out front to scrub her stoop. The paperboy said hi when he passed by, and he had an extra for Margaret today. The stoops always look nice and fresh after you scrub them in the morning. "I scrubbed Larry's this morning too, his and his wife's. I don't mind working, it gives me something to do."

Marg's father came from Sicily, worked stevedore five years, went back for her mother and brought her back. When Marg was growing up they lived over the grocery. Momma raised all the children to be honest and good. No steal, somebody don' have to eat, you give—talked broken. Some of the brothers and sisters are dead now. Vince lives in Baltimore, used to be a captain on the police force. George is dying in a hospital in Florida.

You don't want to look too closely at Marg's legs. All sorts of things, blue, yellow, stuff that'd be covered if people still dressed the way her mother did, if Baltimore was Sicily. Stoop dry now, Marg has a look at the paper. "Tippy listen, what's her name got married again. There was a bad earthquake.

There was some people in a prison over in Africa—didn't say if they was colored or white. The jailers got tired of killing 'em, said okay, youse kill each other. The Taliaferros' girl's boy's in jail for stealing a car. Vince said if he'd only stole twenty he'd've had a suspended sentence. Dagwood never changes."

Another fire already? No, it's an ambulance this time tearing up Lombard Street. "Tippy don't howl at them like some dogs. Good thing, she'd be howling twenty times a day here. Fred must've come from somewhere off this main artery though 'cause look, Tippy, Fred's throwing his head up, will he howl?" No, he's learning.

Marg walks out to the curb. She can see straight down Lombard to downtown. Before they had cars, and before they had so many tall buildings, it was a pretty view down to the harbor. Marg was last down there when she lived up on Hollins Street. She and that nice lady that lived under her used to take a bus downtown almost every Saturday to do some window-shopping. What was that lady's name? It wasn't Teresa. It wasn't Carolyn, what was her name. It wasn't Anna Maria. Sighting down the wide dirty street is like holding those tall downtown buildings between the tips of Marg's lashes. No more ambulances for now.

When she's done with the paper Marg brings out her stepladder and her bucket and rag to wash her front windows. "If we wait long enough maybe somebody'll come along to help us, Tippy. I climbed trees when I was a kid but with my legs like they are now I don't know if I'd do any better with that ladder than you would, Tippy."

Street-level row-house windows in this part of Baltimore have crowds of dolls looking out, artificial flowers, stuffed animals, palm trees and cars, Jesuses and fruit arranged between the glass and the lace to make the house prettier and cheer up people that walk by. Lots need cheering up in this part of Baltimore. Marg used to put nice things in her windows when she'd be on the ground floor. She had a ceramic tree limb with three fat bluebirds on it. For a while she had a liquor bottle shaped like a fiddle. She bought it at the Goodwill store—Marg never touches a drop. Once she had a perfume bottle from the Goodwill too and it was a Spanish lady. She had them all in her window, the fiddle on one side and the bluebirds on the other, like they were making music for the lady.

In a while sure enough out comes Punky and offers to help. "Punky, *please* be careful. I'd never be able to look your mother in the face if you fell and hurt yourself washing my windows. You'll understand what I mean when you have kids of your own."

"That'll be never," says Punky.

"Stay out of Punky's way, Tippy." Tippy's small and looks as if she has some collie in her, always looks sleepy. She stands on the stoop and tilts her head, watching Punky wash Marg's windows. He's a good boy, sixteen, knows everybody in the neighborhood. "Punky, how's your mother this morning? What are youse aiming to do if that landlady sells the house out from under us? I told her I didn't aim to move till my lease was out."

"Lots of luck," says Punky.

"Thanks, Punky, those windows look real nice. Don't they, Tippy."

Vince doesn't drink either, none of Marg's brothers and sisters. Their parents used to drink wine with their dinners, but that was in the old days. They talked Italian with each other. Strict, wouldn't let their children drink wine or smoke. Vince smokes but Marg's never smoked a cigarette. In the old days there weren't so many bars and taverns either. Most of the ones you see now used to be grocery stores (they call them confectioneries). Now they're bars, some of their windows are bricked up.

Outside in the two o'clock heat the marble of the clean steps feels cool under Margaret. She fans herself with one of the fans she got two for a nickel at the Salvation Army store around on Pratt Street. Stiff paper stapled to wood like a big Popsicle stick, and shaped sort of like a Popsicle too. A pale green orchid with rays like the sun and a pale ad for a mortuary up on Baltimore Street, says courteous service in every price range, air-conditioned. Tippy lies in the shadow beside the steps. Up and down the sidewalks, in gutters and in the street broken glass sparkles in the blaze of heat. Marg shades her eyes. Who's that skinny lady crossing the street up there? Is it Lucy?

Lunch was good at the church, beans and franks, slaw. They're not supposed to let animals in the church but Tippy's so good and quiet the nun lets her stay in the vestibule. Today Marg couldn't eat all her beans and the nun let her scrape the plate off in the alley for Tippy.

When the weather's nicer Marg and Tippy take a walk after their lunch but today they just came on home. The pavement was burning Tippy's feet so after a while Marg picked her up and they came the rest of the way like that. Most ground-floor bedrooms are in the back but sometimes an old person has to live in the apartment and they give her the front room, or people watch their TVs in the living room during the day, so sometimes an air conditioner sticks out right over the sidewalk. Water drips out of it and that's good for the dogs and cats, but the air blowing out of it is even hotter than the air in the street. Loretta across the street said her kid brother said some of the new people that are moving into the neighborhood now and buying whole houses and fixing them up and living in them one family to a house like in the old days, said some of those new people have their whole houses air-conditioned. Must be behind their houses, they have the fronts fixed up nice. That'd be nice to have the whole house cool in the summer. Of course you heat up your backyard while you cool down your house, and some of that extra heat could get into other backyards where people don't have air conditioners and have to keep their windows open.

With Tippy under her arm like a purse Marg came on back down Pratt. Both the crab stores were full of people. The Lithuanian bar still has windows and some people were in there, old ones and young ones, drinking beer. It must've been air-conditioned. They must've been talking Lithuanian.

Yes, that is Lucy, bowlegged and skinny, looks like some kind of comedy bird. You can tell Lucy's Irish, there's still some red in her hair. You wouldn't guess she was fifty though. Marg waves, Lucy doesn't see her yet. Irish sticks together as much as Lithuanians but they talk good English. Colored sticks together too. One of Vince's boys drives a city bus and he said there's places that's all colored, don't no white people live there.

"Here, Lucy." Marg gives her the other fan. It's round and more colorful. Lucy says hi to Tippy like they were both arriving at work at some factory and Lucy didn't have time to say more than hi. Tippy didn't wag her tail even when she was a pup.

What was that lady's name though? It wasn't Teresa, it wasn't Catherine. It wasn't Ramona. She wasn't Italian or Irish either. Wasn't Lithuanian or Polack either. What was her name though? It wasn't Leona.

"Hi, Larry. Tippy, say hi to Larry. Lucy, this is my neighbor Mr. Larry."

Colored people live in the house in the alley behind Marg's. Usually Marg doesn't notice them but last Friday they had a picnic in their backyard, barbecued something and for a while in the afternoon it was nice to hear them over the fence when Marg was hanging out her drawers and nightgown she'd washed in the sink—they were having a good time just like a bunch of Italians except you couldn't understand most of what they said. But after dark they got loud. They were drunk and they'd laugh and then they'd get mad and yell out things. You couldn't say anything or they'd break your windows. Mostly they're quiet though. Hi Larry. Lucy, this is my neighbor Mr. Larry. Tippy, say hi to Larry.

Larry back from his law school pats Tippy's head. Him and his wife are nice people. He's a law student, she's a nurse at Mercy. One of their friends lives with them. They all help each other and they mind their own business. Lots of people around, you mention something and before you know it it's in the next block. They'll start rumors on you too. That lady across the street's the worst. Not even married to that man that lives with her. Sits under that tree—only house in the block set back from the sidewalk—all day in her nightgown and one fancy robe or another, eats melon and watches everything like it's hers and then talks about people and if she don't see something for gossip she'll make it up. Just because Marg ain't married and her best friends are women, that lady started a rumor Marg *likes* women. Marg first heard it around the corner, halfway down the other block. She was mad—came back and let that lady know what she thought of her loud enough for plenty to hear. They haven't spoke since. Loretta that lives upstairs next to that lady can't stand her.

Once that lady put a armchair out for the garbagemen to pick up. Loretta and her kids was taking it to use in their place and that lady come out and tried to stop them. She's a pain in the you know what.

Marg likes Larry but once this old man was walking up the street. Walking with canes and he was sick. Marg said rest on my steps a while. Larry comes out and's getting in his car, and Marg says, can you give this man a ride just three blocks up? He's sick and this sun's enough to make anybody weak. Let him take a cab, Larry said. He wasn't himself though, he'd spilled boiling water on his arm and scalded it. Once Marg tipped a cup of coffee onto her and the only thing she could think of was to cool it with cold tap water. The doctors said that was the best thing she could have done. It was like she knew what to do.

But Larry's nice. Sometimes he gives Marg a ride out to the supermarket. Don't worry, she treats him if he lets her, a Popsicle, a bar of soap. If she has to move he'll help her. It makes a difference if you know people you can ask for help.

Most of the people here's always been Lithuanian or Italian. Some Irish and then the colored people. Larry you know the lady youse bought your house from was Lithuanian. She was my landlady. Oh I wish I'd known youse so I could have set you wise. Youse shouldn't've paid fifteen thousand, but how could you know. I remember she came in all excited. Marg glances off toward the sky. Her eyes widen, she leans forward atremble with hope and rubbing her palms together. Big money, oh big money.

"Hi, Miss Margaret."

Hi Teresa, hi Donna. "Girls, this is Mr. Larry. He's gonna be a lawyer. You get in trouble with the law someday, he'll be able to get you out. Violence is one thing, but a woman don't have enough money, she steals a pretty pink dress for her little daughter, how can you hate her for that? Aw, I know it's not sure you could get these girls out but I know you'd try. Larry's Italian. My landlady's Italian though and she don't treat me any better. Oh she had me fooled at first, said Margaret I know you're on welfare. Acted like a friend. Fooled me. So just because you're Italian don't mean you're good. Ain't no guarantee."

Once Loretta from across the street spilled a pot of spaghetti down her legs. She was small then, it was in Highlandtown right after she and Darrel got married. She was wearing short shorts, had to go to the hospital and everybody looked at her with spaghetti all stuck to her legs. Healed up nice, but sometimes when it's cold the spaghetti marks show. Loretta's forty pounds heavier now. Darrel's that much or more. He works, and that lady across the street has started a story Loretta's doing things with some man when Darrel's at work.

"Say hello to the mailman, Tippy. I bet you wish all dogs was as nice as Tippy. I didn't think there'd be any mail for me. I don't guess you remember if you left Lucy anything. Tomorrow everybody'll be waiting for you. Say, if you got sick on welfare-check day would they send somebody else? I know it's against the law to put your hand in somebody else's mailbox, Lucy, but a lady I knew over on Bentalou Street, somebody stole her check right out of her mailbox while she was putting a Band-Aid on her grandchild that had cut itself. I gave her a piece of bread out of every loaf I bought that month. I dieted some that month, you wouldn't know to look at me now. Tippy, be still. Lots gave her bread, I wasn't the only one. I know you're hot Tippy, we'll go in in a minute."

Here comes the donkey cart with fruit and bells. Tippy knows better than to get close to that old donkey. Leroy's the boy with the cart but it belongs to old Mr. Santoni. He's from Naples, not Sicily. Look at the pretty red panaches over the donkey's ears.

"It's too hot to sit on the stoop, Lucy, come inside."

Lucy's husband drinks, Lucy comes down two or three times a day to sit with Marg. Fifty-one, doesn't look forty, skinny, bright red lipstick, vacancy in her eyes from the life she's had. Lucy's none too strong. If Marg moves maybe they won't be seeing each other so much. "What's the matter with your ear, Tippy? Hold still, oh I see it, it's a tick, there, I should have thrown it out but I dropped it on the floor and I trod on it. Merv Griffin was good yesterday. He had a nice singer, looked like Julius LaRosa."

Lucy's voice sounds like a little kid's and she talks fast, says, "I saw Johnny Carson last night. I couldn't sleep, I don't know why, he was snoring to beat the band. I took the TV in the kitchen. I didn't turn no lights on, just opened the windows.

There was some air." Talks like a windup toy, never looks at you.

Since Marg was the baby she stayed home longer than the others, helped her parents and then her mother with the house and grocery. Vince was already started in the police. George and some of the other boys worked in the rail yards and all the girls except Cecilia and Marg were married and raising families already. In '37 they had to sell the grocery. Marg cared for her mother when she fell ill with misdiagnosed cancer. Vince and the other boys arranged for the funeral and said Marg should have what furniture and stuff was left. By then she was too large for most of her mother's clothes so she sold them to people she knew would get some use out of them. Same for the jewelry she had to sell after that. Vince got her a job at a fish stall over in the Hollins Market. The pay wasn't good but she lived on it nine years. Sometimes she'd go to the picture show with one of her girlfriends. That job was hard work but she had a good time. Then the stall owner sold and the new one had children to give the work to. Marg worked nights as a cleaning lady in one of the new buildings downtown. The work was harder and the pay wasn't as good but she did it three years. But by then it was already getting dangerous after dark downtown. One night when she and another cleaning lady were waiting for their bus back to West Baltimore they were robbed by juvenile delinquents. Vince made her quit after that. He tried to find her some other job, in the daytime and closer to home, but they wanted younger people. Marg moved to a cheaper place in Ridgely and sold all the furniture that was any good. There was a bed from Italy. In '67 she got on welfare. By then she'd been living in places near Union Square for some time.

"If I'd've held onto that bed awhile it would've been worth more, I might've got me some teeth. Once, it must be fifteen years ago and it was summer, one morning down on Ostend Street I was going to sit with a lady I knew lived on China

Street, her husband was a glazier. I was walking along and a girl comes out of a corner bar, like to run into me, had a baby under her arm, barefoot, had on cutoffs and a halter and around her neck was one of Momma's necklaces I'd sold to a lady that had died. A chain of butterflies. When Momma dressed up and put on that necklace she'd say, from Firenze, from Firenze. Best *oreficere*, Firenze. Her brother'd bought it for her when she was three.

"If the landlady kicks us out though Tippy we won't have to sleep in the gutter with Fred. A lady two blocks down, off Pratt Street, I saw her today at the lunch at the church and she said she was looking for somebody to rent her top floor. We could live there. It's the house next to the one that has that ad for Country Club Soda painted on the side of it, the one with the different kinds of fruit all in pretty colors."

After supper Margaret walks Tippy and Fred comes along too, into Union Square, a park the size of a block. Tippy heels naturally, Fred runs around more. It's still light out.

Back when Marg was a girl some evenings Poppa and Momma'd bring the kids walking up here through this park. Had real gas street lamps. Poppa said the kids should see how rich folks lived. Then after a while the people with money moved away, kept the houses or sold them, poor people moved in to rent. Now real-estate people have started to buy up houses. They pay more than anybody here could, then sell for twice that to strangers, people like Larry and his wife. They're not bad people but when they move in, those that lived there before have to go. Like that poor Puerto Rican family up the street, four kids and a baby on the way, all on the ground floor, been there going on three years. They fixed the place up, taped pictures on the walls, she made flowers out of colored tissue paper.

Lucy's home frying up a chop. Her husband's at the table. "I'm glad we have our own house," she says. "Hope we can keep it a while, maybe we can. Marg's supposed to be out of her place at the end of the month. I don't know if I could live like that. It's not exactly her fault though. But still."

Larry's wife has washed her hair at their kitchen sink. Afternoon light comes in over the rooftops. Larry's at the table reading a lawbook article about a poor lady that sued a canning company. Their friend's at the supermarket buying dinner. It's a pink sky with a trail from a jet, still hot. Some people start to get off work and then some are waking up and getting ready for night jobs. Larry's wife's drying her pretty brown hair in a towel, leaning against the water heater. Larry turns over his book and starts talking. His wife smiles.

In Union Square Marg's aquiline glance rakes the park and catches Fred finding a place to do his business. Seems like they're keeping up the grass better than they used to. Done with absorbing heat for the day, concrete and brick now need only sigh it back through another short hot night. "Tippy, see that house with the boy leaning out the second-floor window? I used to live there, I loved looking out at the park. What was that lady's name that lived under me there? It wasn't Inez.

"Hi, Mrs. Anderson. She remembers me from when I used to live next-door to her there, always waves. She and Mr. Anderson own their house since 1927 but they didn't get it all paid for till the Second World War. He keep the rooms on the second and third floors locked, she ain't been in some of them in twenty years. She's too old to do anything but put up with it now. Face like a prune. I used to feel sorry for her. He'd take a chair out on their back porch, put a sheet around him and sit there and smoke a cigar and yell at her while she cut his hair. Had to cut the hairs out of his nose too. I don't see how she did it with that cigar smoke blowing in her face. Her eyes was already bad too, looked milky.

"Hey, Fred, I bet you're glad this ain't New York City—they'd put you in jail for doing that.

"If we do move to that upstairs apartment though Tippy

we'll still come back up here sometimes for old times' sake." The new people are changing the houses around the square, sandblasting peeling paint off the brick, washing fanlights, restoring. They strip pilasters and architraves, the cornices with their block modillions, and paint them new colors other than black, new olives and bisques. "I'll have to see that upstairs place before I decide, though. There ain't a real backyard, it's all concrete, but there's two big clotheslines. It's on a alley but it's all white people. The rooms would be smaller but then they wouldn't get so cold in the winter. I'd be saving twenty dollars a month, that's five dollars a week. That's better than half a dollar a day, Tippy. I think I'll do it, I don't need to stay where I'm not wanted. Larry'll help me move, and Mike that lives with him and his wife. Punky'll help. Lucy'll help me get things ready to move and help me put things around in the new place. Hey, Fred, will you come down there to visit me and Tippy?

"I can still climb stairs. Good exercise." Slowly, her bulk filling the well, negotiating the turn.

The longest stair Marg ever climbed was to the top of the shot tower over east of downtown when she was ten. It was a Sunday afternoon, summer like now but not such a heat. Momma and Poppa took Margaret. The tower's like a big smokestack with a stairway inside. It had been built for some war, not the Great War but an earlier one. From the top you looked down inside and saw how they let molten lead drip and fall all that way down into tubs of water to make ammo.

You could also look out over Baltimore, see the harbor and the boats at the docks, the different churches, the train yards, the parks including Union Square surely. Of course it mustn't have been as big as now, but it was so much bigger than Margaret had expected, she felt as if Sicily, Ireland and Lithuania must be out there beyond Fort McHenry. Poppa pointed toward Nanticoke Street, said see, Margaret, there's our house. She'd nodded but she really hadn't seen it, it was too small, there were too many houses, she tried but she couldn't. Poppa'd said wave, Margaret, wave to our house, maybe Vincente's looking out the window. She couldn't find the house so she'd waved to all the houses.

Most of the Union Square trees are ginkgoes. Once many varieties grew across North America and elsewhere, but the last ice age rendered them extinct, all but the one variety that survived in China by human intercession, venerated and tended in temple grounds through the centuries. These here are descendants of those Chinese ones. They are tall and seem to strain upward in the hot dusk.

That old man on the bench lives next to the Andersons. His story's a long one, but then everybody's is. Marg waves to him as she moves through the park past the dry fountain, talks a minute with somebody on the corner. All these people have their different stories. The row houses have stories and stories reaching back to before Marg was born and farther, and Marg knows many of those. What was that nice lady's name though? It wasn't Ramona, it wasn't Thelma. Around Union Square the houses stand in twos and threes like forty Andrews Sisters singing cheek to cheek for Margaret and Tippy and Fred under the tall ginkgoes in the last light.

Retrieval

The lawnmower's ready, a reminder for Jessye about next month's PTA, then Jessye from her folks' house (her dad's Wurlitzer in the background), the flight no problem, Jason's already on the beach, we miss you already, don't wait a week, come sooner, the beep, and then: "Hey, Rob," and then a long pause for me to try to place the burred male voice, "come on go fishing this weekend." I could have retrieved the messages from work but I don't know, with the house empty it gave me something to look forward to.

The things that cross the mind of a nearly forty-year-old software designer in north Atlanta six-thirty after bad traffic a hot June Thursday in an empty house, waiting for the recognition of a somehow forgiving and older male voice to come, if it will come. My only child Jason on the white Florida sand in his skimpy bathing suit with its pattern of naked women. Jason pushing puberty and surely ogled there on the beach, striding into the shining waves. Me at eight or ten alone on a Carolina beach a bit later in the year and in the day, me and the sand crabs watching incoming waves stand up and reflect the setting sun under a darker eastern sky. Earlier, fishing those waves on Dad's boat, my cousin Blake just graduated from Vandy and visiting us at the end of his honeymoon, landlubbler Blake doing his best to gut a big one on the foredeck while Dad smoked his pipe at the wheel. Is Jessye right that we're all old boys at heart or do fortieth birthdays do that to us as they approach? Not that it matters, we do what we're programmed for unless there's a glitch.

My tape won't register the ghosts of other conversations I knew were there on the line, but in the pause I did hear the man breathe a kind of sigh. It made me recognize him, so that aloud, but more to myself than to him, I said, "Blake. What's happening." I could feel the air as it kicked on, and I shook my head.

Cousin Blake and I had seen each other maybe four times in our lives. He edited a music-industry weekly in Nashville, was ten years widowered with a couple of grown children, maybe grandkids. After identifying himself he went on to say a pal had had to withdraw from a fishing trip the two of them had set up for this weekend at a lake on the Tennessee-Kentucky border. I should fly to Nashville Thursday if possible, otherwise Friday, rent a car and follow the directions he gave me, and save receipts so he could put me on his expense account. He himself would be gone by four, there by six. The camp office had a phone in case I got lost, but they'd have instructions not to relay any messages to Blake. "So then Rob my man, your old cousin'll be looking for you. They rent poles and gear in case maybe you don't have yours handy. Tear yourself away, Rob—it'll do us both a world of good." Beep, more odds and ends, then the nearly silent tape that wound by for a good minute before I shut it off with a little shiver, because of the breeze on my neck but also because I saw that my mind was already made up.

At the save time I knew that if I really was an old boy at heart, it was mostly in the company of my wife, or alone. Now that I thought about it, as my scout-troop venture into the Dismal Swamp and Carolina soccer halftimes gave way to business meetings and club golf and showers a certain distaste persisted in the pleasure of those episodes. When only men are there it somehow smells like tennis shoes. You like the horrible smell, but it makes you think of reading Fleers waxed comics, the wad in your cheek, your trusty slingshot tucked in your belt. Maybe what taints that regress is its incompleteness. Maybe with your wife you go all the way back and so pass that whiff of shame. Damned if it doesn't make you wonder whether "growing up" isn't taking the easy way out. Well, and then of course other questions arose—what did Blake want from me, what kind of shape was the guy in anyway?

Nashville's another world, you see at one in the morning when you tool in to an airport closing up shop for the night. An hour later when you pull off onto the shoulder for a peek at the directions and map, when you switch off the dome light you're almost tempted to switch off the heads too. The windows are open. Some kind of field leans out to what looks like a pair of cooling towers on the horizon. On the windshield a lightning-bug smear still glows. There must be tobacco and cows out there. Down a gravel drive a dark farmhouse stands in the violet of its utility light. Even in north Atlanta you don't have quiet like this.

It was Friday morning. I'd taken the day off with a message to the office answering machine. I planned to surprise Jessye and Jason in the afternoon with a call from the fishing camp. Rather than root for equipment in the back of the garage I'd taken Blake's word it was rentable. Now I sat with my carry-on bag and a bottle of Tennessee whiskey in the Avis Century, checking the map. Before leaving home I'd noted my destination on the memo pad beside the kitchen phone. I was on a two-lane road by now. Other than the tractor a while back there hadn't been traffic. Just past ten, the dash clock said, and my watch agreed.

It was eleven when I pulled up to the camp office. You couldn't see the water yet but you could feel its slight pressure on your skin, and you could sure smell it, like inferior metal, and you could hear frogs.

The camp office, a cinder-block shed with a rusty Orange Crush thermometer beside the door, made me feel easier about Blake's expense account. The slow towhead at the counter explained that he was there for night fishing, and that Blake earlier had settled in in houseboat number two, half a mile down the gravel-becoming-dirt road that led through the woods past driveways to five cabins—light from one of them showing between the trees, and quiet laughter—to the shore and past the way to the first houseboat, which seemed unoccupied. The road ended where it turned left into the little opening where I parked beside Blake's five- or six-year-old dark Pontiac. Nobody I knew drove an American car. I shut off my lights and engine and got out. By then I was tired. I closed the car door and just stood there. I could see kerosene light from the cabin of the houseboat down at the end of a short dock, and the night was clear enough for me to make out the still water stretching out beyond. The loud frogs somehow made the night quieter. The water smelled loud too. "Fresh" water, but it smelled like used bandages to me. I'd crossed the gangplank to the narrow starboard deck when I heard a low growl just to my right. Then farther on, from the foredeck, "Hush up Blue. Rob I hope that's you boy." A chair scraped, and the boat moved a little as Blake came down to me. Blue pushed past between me and the cabin wall, snuffling me as he went. Blake and I shook hands in the dark. "Robbie. I knew you could do it. I didn't have a second's doubt."

So okay we went down into the lighted cabin and grinned and shook hands again and broke out the whiskey for a couple of three-fingers. We told each other how good we were looking of course, even though in fact we'd both put on more weight than we needed, and Blake struck me right away as having let himself go a little to seed, and he limped. How's the family, how's business, how's Nashville, Atlanta—

black Blue lay on one of the lower bunks and watched us sail through these preliminaries into a calm. It was after two when we undressed and turned in. Get us some good ones tomorrow.

I slept until nine, later than in years. I woke to water light moving on the ceiling. The mixed smells of lake water, cabin and head, dog, coffee and cold eggs almost made me think I was bivouaced with my National Guard platoon, except . . . except I could hear deep silence spreading out in all directions beyond earshot. I'd have to have missed reveille, the platoon was in the next county and they hadn't turned around yet. Jessye by now would have recovered from a wild night of bingo, she'd have made something with béchamel for breakfast, she and her parents would have sent Jason to the beach in his risqué bathing suit and now they'd have taken second or third cups out onto the deck. I stretched.

I shaved, although I'd have liked not to, shaved because I didn't know whether Blake would have shaved or not and I didn't want to be more informal than my host. He'd somehow got up, not shaved, made breakfast and disappeared for Blue's morning walk while I slept. So I only got to skip one morning, because Sunday I had to shave for the trip back into civilization. In the empty cabin I pulled on my jogging shorts and polo shirt and slid into my flip-flops.

Eggs and toast, coffee from a thermos, and somehow a local paper on the deal table at the window. A prom queen held court under a decorated backboard alongside a muted account of new deaths from the Chernobyl accident. Out on the lake a fish jumped. I washed and stowed the dishes and went out for a look around. The far shore was closer than I'd expected, wooded except for a cleared space with three cows and what looked like a house trailer. The lake seemed to meander around bends both to the left and right and indeed I heard the buzz of an outboard and then saw the boat with its single fisherman push into view from the far left and then shut off and coast under the trees across the lake. Our own outboard floated behind the houseboat. The day looked as if it would be hazy and mild.

Before long Blake came over the gangplank with Blue. They'd walked to the office to pick up some beers and sandwiches for lunch, bait, and fishing gear for me. We stowed the supplies and gear and set out around the bend to the right past woods and pastures to a spot Blake had fished before. By the time we'd anchored and set the lines it must have been two or three, and I was hungry enough for even the camp office's submarines to taste good, and the cold beer was better. It was time for us to start looking at each other.

Blake shifted and swigged a beer. "So then Rob. The computers seem to be treating you okay. What you driving these days? Your outfit laying off any? Lordy, lordy, Rob, I still remember fishing off your daddy's boat. You see they put Johnny Paycheck away? But I'll tell you this, blood's thick, does my heart good to see how good that computer company's treating you, Rob. It's the future—we got PC franchises opening up in every Nashville shopping center, like you must have down in Atlanta. You like Tammy Wynette? People say Kenny Rogers must think somebody has a contract out on him, he travels with so much security." Blake beamed a sallow smile my way. "Say though, you growing up when you did, I'm wondering how much country you ever really knew. Don't lie, you probably must have thought the British invasion would last into the next century, didn't you. No offense, times change. Country changes, but no invasion'll ever vanquish it. Country *assimilates*, know what I mean, Rob?"

I wasn't sure I did so I asked what kind of fish we were likely to get. The lake had opened out again and we'd anchored in the middle to trawl over a submerged village. The hazy sun didn't make it far into the turbid water, but I could see the tops of some trees a few yards below the surface. When two men haven't seen each other for a while, trying to catch up can be tricky. You process and store what he has to say and how he says it, how he handles himself—how well he casts line and the tremor as he lifts half a sub for a bite. I guess you want to know if he's still on an even keel. You watch how his Lab watches a dragonfly hover over the tackle box and then glances up at you.

Blake said, "Black bass, smallmouth, walleye, crappie. Some stocked brown trout and bluegill. They say there's muskie but I don't know about that." He was wearing old Topsiders, new, good khakis and a tan checked shirt. He wore one of those black watches with more functions than anybody needs. I didn't remember the liver spots on the backs of his hands. "But so anyway, Rob, you and Jessye ought to bring Jason to see Nashville sometime. I could get him some autographs if he likes country music. He must be, what, eight or nine? No, thirteen? I can't believe it. You take him fishing?"

Once six years before, off the Outer Banks. Jessye hadn't wanted me to, and then had had to come along. When the bluefish we'd reeled in on Jason's line lay gasping on the deck, Jason had asked was it a baby whale. I inquired after Blake's kids and professed approval when I learned that one taught school and one sold insurance. We threw back most of what we caught that afternoon and evening, and motored back with a slim string of the introduced trout for dinner. Fog was easing out from the trees onto the lake surface, like something on MTV in black and white. In the bottleneck a canoe with a stern lantern met and passed us. "Anything biting out there?" While Blake cleaned and battered the fish, Blue and I jogged back to the camp office for me to call Florida. Jessye was amazed to hear where I was. Jason told what the Marine World dolphins had been capable of that noon, and wished I'd hurry on down so we could see Disney World again. Then

Jessye again, about my excursion: you let them out of your sight for a minute, and see. Be careful, Rob. (Mmm.) But not too careful.

What in the world could she have meant by that, I wondered, though all I said was, okay but it's you guys have the Atlantic in your faces. As we returned in the dark Blue preceded me but wasn't much help as a guide. I relied on a trick I'd learned in scouts. Instead of trying to search out your footing or the adjacent vegetation you keep your eyes forward and unfocused. You negotiate without difficulty. Under the dim utility light Blue crossed the gravel and the gangplank, his heavy shoulder blades shuttling.

"What the hell is it you want from me Blake I'm wondering, buddy," I said as I lifted the good bourbon and branch waiting at my place at the table. "I haven't been treated this good since I don't know when, maybe my honeymoon."

Blake was shaking one of the trouts in a paper bag. "You'll do the same for me sometime. Where was your honeymoon? You remember I wound mine up fishing with you in Carolina. Only time in my life I ever went ocean fishing." He threw a smile over his shoulder at me.

It made us even, I said, since I'd never fished in anything but salt water, and not that since I was grown. I listened to the frogs and the dot-matrixing insects, and felt the cold whisky hit my stomach, warmth start to bloom from it.

Blake said, "I guess we don't want to get too even about this though, do we." His back was to me, but I could see that he must have been kind of gazing down into the pan of butter and trout, and he stopped shaking the pan for a second or so. When I allowed as how he'd have to run that one by me again he first gave his head a little shake no, and then a bigger shake, and then he said, "I mean I wouldn't want to divvy my arthritis up with you, Rob." I let it go.

We switched to beers with the trout, and I sopped up more of the pan drippings than I really needed with slices of Wonder Bread. Blake told me more about Nashville and about Nashville personalities. Dolly Parton bless her heart was as unpretentious as she seemed, Minnie Pearl had more money than she knew what to do with, compact disks would soon be the only format.

"Until the next one comes along," I said. I talked some about accelerating computer technology and market saturation, foreign competition. We talked about the Russian nuclear accident, about the space-shuttle disaster, some about baseball, some even—a little, just a word here and there, a look—about our estimates of the world's chances of reaching the next century. I washed the dishes and we turned in early, since Saturday we meant to fish in earnest. Blake set the alarm for four.

Blake's breathing slowed and quietened. I thought Blue in the bunk below was asleep too, but I couldn't be sure. The sky had cleared outside and water lights from the new moon came in the houseboat windows and moved on the white ceiling. I tried to remember whether I had ever met Blake's parents. I thought not, no, just his new wife that time on their honeymoon, and I could barely remember her as a buxom letter sweater—she must have been the first "coed" I'd ever seen. I started to roll over toward the dark interior of the bunk and the movement jarred loose more memories.

The morning before Blake's and his wife's arrival I had passed the doorway of the bedroom guests always used and seen my father's legs protruding from under the cherry four-poster I had thought of as an heirloom, it was so seldom used, though now as I saw it in my mind's eye I realized it must have come from Sears to be part of my mother's trousseau. I watched my father's legs twitch and one rise into the air exactly as when he worked under our Ford. Then I asked what he was doing. He invited me to slide under for a look. With his pocketknife he had cut into the center of the cream muslin underlining of the box springs and torn out a handkerchief-sized square of it that lay with the knife on his chest. He had looped heavy twine up into the opening and over the metal frame that supported the mattress, and was tying an exaggerated bow in the loop that hung a couple of inches below the springs, weighted with a brass cat's bell. I asked the obvious question, and my father explained that it was a trick we were playing on Blake and his wife. He turned his head sideways on the dustless waxed floor to look at me. I must have been six or seven and my father thirty.

He must have watched to see me fail to understand the surprisingly elaborate joke. And I guess I must have seen a patience I recognized as meaning there were deeper waters here we could wade into if I chose. Surely I chose not to—in fact I don't think I ever waded into those waters with my father, any more than Jason has yet done with me.

But I suppose something about the moment must have made me curious about what Blake's wife would be like because now I remembered sitting beside her in chilly sunshine—it would have been on the back porch three blocks inland, gulls crying and the flag snapping over the house—sitting beside her to watch with interest the valentine-red polish glide over her toenails. Funny, I thought, and was turning to bury my face in the pillow when the system coughed up two more memories, these not so funny.

I saw my mother setting a covered enameled orange casserole she held with potholders onto a trivet on the dining table at supper. She had come from the kitchen doorway behind Blake who sat across from me. His wife was at my left, and my father down at the end. My eyes seemed to be the only ones raised in the room. The moment was troubled.

And then one last memory told me what the trouble had been. The memory came because I was giving up the way I do in the last consciousness before sleep. I think I understood it fully in that glimmering. Coming as it did then, this recollection maintained a peculiar status through the rest of the weekend. I thought of it only two or three times, in passing, the way you remind yourself—oh yes, I forgot—that a friend has cancer now, something fairly grave that won't bear discussing and about which you can do nothing. I think the recollection held this status because the access it gave me was more to my father than to either Blake or me. It came in an image and an understanding. The image was of Blake in his orange life vest, a fraternal and protective smile leaving his face as my father's boom swung around to strike him across the chest and send him overboard. And the image was of my father at the tiller winking to me. I seemed to lean forward to follow Blake's shocked and supplicating face over the side of the boat. My father had come about without warning, a trick I'd seen only the youngest and greenest sailors play, and the wink had been to make me complicit. Except that now in the houseboat bunk I thought I remembered somehow not going along—maybe not winking back—because of what I had understood.

My father had lived and did live a good life, I think, working hard seining and making a good living at it, loving my mother, raising me. Out on the Carolina coast there hadn't seemed any reason for resentment of anybody, and I had arrived at my tenth year supposing that the kind of life we led there would always be available because it was immutable. Probably my father had believed much the same thing most of his life, and so had his brother, whatever job it was had taken him inland. But change was starting to leach in. Here was this nephew with his new wife (I hadn't seen her yet in my memory of the shipboard incident, but I knew she was on board and saw it happen too) talking about Vanderbilt. It wasn't enough that he botched gutting a mackerel. His new wife—with the Vandy privileges my mother had never had either—this coed might have been unable to appreciate what a butchering her new husband was giving the fish. He might afterwards have been able to make it out to be some kind of triumph in her eyes. My poor father with his bird's breastbone and skimpy tidewater book learning abandoned for the sea he loved and even trusted, he must have known it was wrong but couldn't help himself, he had to take Blake down a notch in his new wife's sight.

My father got more than he bargained for, I thought, as a few more pictures surfaced when I rubbed my forehead across the rough pillow—Blake thrashing in the water, shivering on deck in his wife's arms (here she was), my mother's downcast eyes that evening at supper.

What I remembered clearest though—and this most of all through the next day and a half felt like something Blake and I had acknowledged to each other for what it was—was Blake's surprise as the boom swung into him, surprise at my father's betrayal of his trust, and also at my betrayal for not warning him when I saw my father sweep the tiller around. I turned my head over on the pillow. I could see fireflies at the window from time to time, with their measured signals too dim to reflect off the ceiling.

"All the good times is over and gone, little darlin' don't weep no more," Blake said when he stepped out of the head the next morning at four-thirty and saw me sitting on the edge of my bunk, still befuddled in the kerosene light. "Do us some real fishing today." Half an hour later in the first light and frog silence we and Blue clambered aboard the motorboat and set out with what seemed a great deal of noise. I asked how on a Saturday this fisherman's paradise could be so empty. Did they know something we didn't?

We anchored in a new cove and almost as soon as we had lines in the water the fish were striking. For a couple of hours, before the sun got high enough to slow them, we were too busy to talk much. No musky but we each had a fair string to clean and filet back at the houseboat before icing some down and frying up the others for lunch. We ate outside in deck chairs, plates balanced on knees, beers on the deck beside us. Before I knew what was happening, Blake had eased us into more talk about my company. I looked to Blue for guidance.

Blake said to relax, he wasn't aiming to change careers at this late date. "Nashville's been good to me, country music's been. And I don't know anything more challenging than trade journalism. I was wondering about your prospects, is all. I guess about the future of computers too. Do you make those talking cash registers? What about obsolescence? My neighbors bought a PC so their kids wouldn't grow up behind the times. That was two years ago. Already their kids want fancier games and to get them Steve's shelling out for a new system, know what I mean? CDs are here to stay though, I heard Dolly on one last week. I grant you, some people have sentimental attachments to their record players. Seeing that tone arm ease down on vinyl has to be a touchstone for our era, wouldn't you say? Antique value's bound to accrue too. We bought a Grundig with short wave for the den in '70, big sucker. Now I don't play it, I just like the way it looks. Rob, . . ." Here it came, a request for a loan, cancer in the limping leg, talk about the dead wife. Blue looked up to see my reaction. But all systems were down, as if my recollection last night had sent a spike down the line and I wasn't protected. "Don't know who fileted this one." I lifted a fish bone off my lip. "Yeah Blake?" Here it came. "You were saying? Hey, Blue." A plastic pint crate of strawberries sat on the window sill, white mildew starting to finger out from the impacted bottom. I pushed back and forth the loose skin over Blue's skull. Nothing. I glanced at Blake. He was drawing pictures on the chair arm with water off the side of his beer. "I forgot," he said. A reprieve.

We napped and then bestirred ourselves to motor out to our first spot for a last stint over the submerged hamlet. It was still good fishing weather, overcast and mild. The bad metal taste of the lake air had given way to something sweet and powdery, like five-and-dime cosmetics, or like frogs as I imagined them. I thought I recognized a cow from the day before on the cleared hillside. As we fished (with only fair luck as it turned out) I tried to lure back out whatever it was my cousin had on his mind, and eventually, just before we cranked again to head home, he seemed to come back to the point. It was the last thing I would have guessed. I had been softening him up, I thought, easing us back into the backslapping mode by saying what I knew about Waylon Jennings. "Okay if I talk a little business?" Blake said.

The business was simple enough. His trade paper wanted to computerize for an integrated system between keyed and camera-ready copy and Blake, bless his heart, had thought of me. We talked figures and I said I was pretty sure I could swing a discount for a family member and friend and bulwark of country music. "Don't bother, Rob. You're good to think of it but, hey, I wouldn't see any of the gravy, my business doesn't work like that, not for a man nudging up to retirement anyway, know what I mean?" He had stood and turned to crank the motor. He was already in position, with his left foot braced against the edge of the seat, his left hand on the hump of the big Evinrude, his right gripping the pull rope toggle. He spoke over his shoulder, looking out across the water.

"What's the point then?" I said quickly, to get it in before the engine started. Too quickly. I saw what the point was before Blake said anything—and maybe he was giving me an extra beat to see what the answer had to be and then call up some kind of frame for what I'd said that would convert it into something different. Nothing came though. I put my palms on the seat and pushed my fingers under my thighs and hoped Blake wouldn't look all the way around at me. When Jason is older I want to tell him about this so he can learn from his father's blunder. The lesson is, take your time when what you're talking about matters at all. Surely not too hard to swallow, but with it goes a sadder lesson I'll probably leave unsaid with Jason, a lesson about being men. I'll leave it unsaid because I won't want to authorize it exactly as I pass it along. I'll want Jason to be able to be as free as he can to limit it to a description of his one old man's peculiarities. The lesson is that there was nothing for me to find in that extra beat Blake gave me. With Jessye I must lose it as bad or worse several times a week even after all the years of marriage, and when I was growing up it must have happened about daily with mother. But it's never mattered. With them and one or two other women in my life my slowness and shortsightedness have always had a kind of automatic advance pardon I was glad to rely on. It's really only with other men that I've painted myself into corners, and felt the hollow that grows in your belly when you look up and see what you've done.

Blake said, "I thought maybe your people would be different. One of us ought to be able to get something out of this deal." He pulled and the motor coughed to life. *Sillon*, the furrow from my college French came back for some reason as we slapped across the silver water. Blue balanced on the bow alert for sharks or pirates.

Blake and Blue rode in with me to the camp office the next morning, where the sleepy towhead helped us find out we hadn't broken any records and provided me with an insulated carton and ice for my half of the catch. Blake would walk back to the houseboat and get in another half-day before he drove home. It was hot and the water was smelling sick again. I had a good idea of the system Blake's paper needed and names of contacts there, and I'd given him the name of our person who'd do the designing if the deal went through. So we said good-bye beside the Century. Best weekend I'd had in I couldn't remember when, thanks again, how is it we let so much time slip past without looking each other up, we'll be looking for you in Atlanta next summer, you too Blue. "Okay, Robbie buddy. Glad you could see your way clear to keep an old cousin company for a weekend. You take care now. Drive carefully, hear."

I'd been watching Blue look back and forth between us. I looked up at Blake's whiskered face and straight into his pale blue eyes. If ever the ball was in my court, it was then. I said, "I'm glad you had life vests for both of us here."

Blake nodded. "They're clumsy at first but you get used to them. And you never know."

"Neither of us went overboard this time, though, did we."

"Came through dry," Blake said. "Okay, Rob, you better start hauling it on down that road now."

"Right." We gave each other a light hug and then I got into the car and drove away, down the two-lane through the fields of corn and tobacco and soybeans, past the cooling towers shimmering like a mirage on the horizon, through airwaves full of nothing but ads, news, and country music, to the Nashville airport. Security seemed tighter than I remembered from Thursday, but the paper I bought for the plane ride didn't explain anything. As I pulled in the driveway just at four the impulse sprinkler went into operation, giving me a kind of lazy welcome. Among the mail a postcard from Jason—the two past summers he'd sent pictures of rockets, but this was of the Daytona 500, and said his grandparents had a new Chihuahua who had tried to bite him. It didn't take me long to find Jessye on the Phone-mate, welcome back, be sure to freeze the fish, don't call, Mom and Dad have decided to take Jason and me along to their square-dancing class tonight, talk tomorrow, we miss you, love.

During the week I did get some credit at work for putting Blake's deal in motion, and I did what I could to keep his name visible for whatever good it might do him. It was a fast thin kind of week I passed shaking off some lingering questions—why just now for the reconciliation, was he putting affairs in order, was it cancer in the leg after all?—and coming to see a couple of things about myself. I depend on women to forgive me but forgiveness is not something I want from other men. It works the other way too. Jessye sometimes makes some false steps, Mother must have made some, but they don't matter, they're pardoned in advance and I forget them. But I'd papered over how my father had treated Blake because it did matter. Blake's unwelcome forgiveness had forced an acknowledgment—this is something my father did, and this is why—that didn't feel very much like pardon. Toward the end of that thin week I saw that I'd had enough of the loneliness of men alone together to last me a good long time.

They all drove up to Daytona to meet my plane. Jessye's parents beamed and welcomed me back to their retirement heaven. Jessye's mother's moustache jabbed me in the lip, and she said she couldn't wait for me to meet Tinker Belle "with an *e* because she's so precious, but she still gets carsick so we left her watching 'Miami Vice.'" Jessye's dad had learned a dozen new Wurlitzer numbers since Christmas. It was okay, it was what I wanted.

Jessye slipped an arm under mine and up across my back. A touch down the fronts of our bodies, a touch of lips, a peck under my ear, and who I was and wanted to be came all the way back up, I was talking to my mainframe again and none of those maverick circuits Blake had spooked up would cause any more trouble. Jason in his flowered jams told me he'd worn his digital watch in swimming with no problem. He sidled over, so I could put an arm around his shoulders. Day before yesterday he'd seen dolphins in the ocean.

Playing for Keeps

1. Friends and Lovers

Chance brings Yannic Demombynes back to Montréal in the fall of 1975. He has been traveling haphazardly for almost four years in the United States, Mexico, and Colombia, and living more by odd jobs than by the munificence of his father, a B.C. lumber baron. The man's surgery brings Yannic home and, after the polyps prove benign and Yannic stays on a month to let the family see that he is still sound of mind and body (indeed sounder for the travel, he thinks), and that he still loves and respects them (the more, and not simply because of the long absence but also because their unquestioning faithfulness to an inherited way of life now touches him the more), and that he persists in his decision not to enter the family business, he returns to the Montréal of his student years. There at the Bread and Roses Café he meets Jeremy Stein and Jacquot Loubet. The three are in their late twenties.

The café has been founded and run by a loose group of activists, mostly francophone and mostly ex-students, as a refuge and meeting place for young men from south of the border who have chosen to emigrate rather than take part in their nation's undeclared war in Indochina or be imprisoned for their refusal. Jeremy is one such draft resister. Jacquot, a native Montréaler, is one of the Canadians who wait tables and tend bar, donating their time as a way of supporting the U.S. nationals

Jeremy has grown up in a Cleveland Russian Jewish neighborhood. His grandmother knows only a few words of English but his parents have assimilated to the point that Jeremy himself growing up learned what little he knows of his cultural heritage not from his family but from playmates and from the old people who came into his father's pharmacy, speaking Yiddish, Russian, Hungarian. "For a long time I thought being Jewish, which I knew I was, just meant having grandparents or parents who spoke incomprehensible languages. Or a single language, because I didn't distinguish among them at first, or distinguish them from Hebrew which I heard at a cousin's bat mitzvah and then at my bar mitzvah. When I began to know there were Sephardic and Reformed and other kinds of Jews I thought each group must have its own language, Hungarian, Yiddish, from time immemorial. It was a surprise to learn that Hebrew was a real language, and not a kind of scat talking.

"The neighborhood was a good place for growing up, especially Dad's drugstore. Four wire-backed chairs and two marble-topped tables, for tea and ice-cream sodas. The stockroom was in the cellar. Goods on some of the shelves must have been half a century old. It communicated with other cellars along the street via a tunnel under the sidewalk. I was in the tunnel only once." Jeremy remembered it at the University of Chicago, when his family had moved to a suburb near a new hospital complex where his father had a new more profitable pharmacy with no soda fountain. Jeremy, drawn into a student prank that entailed negotiating university tunnels, recalled the tunnel the old stockroom gave onto, and wondered whether he had imagined or dreamed it, and didn't know until his next visit home.

"Dad said it was real, and even then it felt as if I'd imagined it. The U.S. antiwar underground feels the same way to me."

That network below the border could enable Jeremy to resist arrest indefinitely there, but he has chosen emigration instead of life on the lam. He phones and writes his parents and sister and brother freely, and they're able to visit him without endangering anybody.

Jacquot Loubet works in the resistance café as much to fill up some time as to support the young foreigners' war resistance. Tickling the ivories past four hours a day would take him into the region of diminishing returns—now, anyway—and now that the goal of transforming himself into a professional musician is beginning to seem tenable he wants not to dishearten himself with bad pacing, and so it's good to have something to do in off-hours besides reading, flirting, and daydreaming. Jacquot has grown up in the Montréal university environment. His father is a distinguished professor of history and his mother, a lapsed poet, teaches creative writing. For Jacquot and his older sister (now doing CBC news in Alberta) it has been a pleasant upbringing, and Jacquot is inclined to assume that, allowing for differences between history and music and for differences between generations, he will keep a foothold in his parents' community even if (fingers crossed) he manages to sell himself as some kind of pianist, probably jazz.

Jacquot is qualified to teach music but he hasn't been able to find an institutional niche for himself. He rather enjoys the enforced vacation of unemployment, which reminds him of his parents' periodic sabbatical leaves. He is also enjoying not living with a woman. At first it needed some adjusting when, at the time he was beginning not to find a job, he and his woman of two years separated, she to seek her fortune as an interior decorator in Japan, he to continue not finding work in Montréal, to flirt with other women, go to dinner, make love without letting anything much develop. It's a way to live, it's a change. Money is running out though. Jacquot has considered giving private voice and piano lessons, dismal as that would probably be.

Yannic and Jeremy meet at one of the chessboards at the café. Both play competently and with some flair. After Jeremy's victory they play back through the interesting junctures to see other ways the game might have gone. They walk to Yannic's apartment, Jeremy stops in for a nightcap, and somewhat to their mutual surprise they spend the rest of the night making love, talking, and making love again. The next week Yannic moves in with Jeremy. Both seem to have fallen in love for the first time in their adult lives. They continue to spend odd afternoons and evenings in the café and when Jacquot begins to work there he joins them in chess and talk, and the three begin to meet for the occasional dinner or morning stroll. When Jacquot pinch-hits for a friend in a trio at a jazz club, Jeremy and Yannic form the nucleus of his claque.

Jacquot learns he has inherited, as part of the settlement of the estate of a favorite bachelor uncle, the premises of an out-of-business restaurant in the city of Québec. He is arranging to sell it to finance another couple of years of unemployment when it strikes him that it might be interesting to give restaurateuring a try with his two friends from the café. At least it's worth driving up to Québec to have a look at the place, they decide.

In Québec, when they find the cul de sac in the *basse ville*, Jeremy opines that the location may have something to do with the restaurant's previous failure. A grimy Molson calendar inside shows that the place has stood idle for five years. The only other furnishing in the short lobby is the dusty glass case the cash register must have stood on, displaying cobwebs and an empty rose-colored Swisher Sweets cigar box. The name makes Cleveland Jeremy Smile. He explains why to the francophones in his yet balky Québecois. Tables and chairs remain in the dining area, and some equipment in the kitchen. The cellar seems dry. Two empty floors above the restaurant could provide space for living or storage. "It makes you wonder, though," Jacquot says, "who in the world would have been crazy enough to have tried to make a go of it in the first place. Or how Uncle Jules got suckered into acquiring it." Before they lock up, Yannic draws a heart with his finger in the dust on the glass of the door.

No one speaks for half an hour in the car as they drive back to Montréal. They have almost no business experience and little capital apart from Yannic's familial fortune. Certainly taking on the restaurant would be a waste of good energy, thought, money, and time, and if they wanted to throw themselves away, why not do it in Cartagena or some other tropical place? Québec is charming—Jeremy hasn't seen it before—and the street itself has a certain charm perhaps, but a joke of a restaurant can be opened anywhere, and there are other kinds of jokes too. Yannic leans back, rumpling his sandy curls. "But maybe we should do it anyway." Jeremy sighs, "I . . . think maybe . . . yes." Jacquot at the wheel says, "Okay, then. Let's." Yannic adds, "Chance of a lifetime."

2. *Décor*

The trio must make many decisions about the restaurant. The menu should be distinctive but not quirky, expensive enough to draw patrons from beyond the immediate neighborhood yet not so expensive as to exclude the neighborhood altogether. There are governmental functionaries to deal with, such as the health and sanitation inspectors: is it customary to bribe them? and, if so, with what periphrases does one broach the subject most gracefully? There are the hours: only dinner to start, six to ten Tuesday through Sunday. Sunday brunch the next step if all goes well, then daily lunch, and the dinner hour might need altering too. There is the question of additional personnel. Keep the number of tables small and the menu limited, hire say two more for waiting and busing, take it from there. And there is what they recognize as much the most vital subject, the décor. It subsumes everything in a sense, including menu, clientele, and salaries. It includes the name they have chosen, Tonton Jules.

Since décor will finally be the making or breaking of the restaurant, the three agree not to stint capital outlay for it, and they decide to do nothing—not buy a single potted fern, not wash a single window—until they have talked over the décor-to-be at length. They set aside a day and a night in the lower apartment above with cold cuts, cheese, a radio, and plenty of paper, pencils, and pens. Their voices echo in the empty room, and most of the time it is raining outside.

During the first eight hours, morning and afternoon in the somber changing light they play with hundreds of ideas. Ironies and reductios ad absurdum abound, laughter that quietens gradually. By sunset that phase of their deliberations ends. They sit and lie on the bare floor with rucksacks and jackets as pillows, and grow increasingly aware of the premises extended beneath as a quite real and near enclosed space that has waited unaffected by their play.

"Hmm . . ."

Yannic wears a blue sweat suit. He rumples his ginger curls and smiles. "Décor . . . implies intentionality. We want to give the place a décor. Which is to say that at the moment it's without one, no?"

Jacquot shrugs. "Or an incomplete one, or the ruins and relics of one that's not exactly to our taste."

"Check." There is no music, the rainy windows darken.

Yannic says, "But if instead we take it as intentional exactly now, exactly as it is. If we suppose that we've hired the best of all decorators—"

"Your Claire, Jacquot."

Jacquot looks heavenward, shaking his head.

Yannic continues, "Right, she's won the Nobel Prize for decorating and we bring her back from Japan for Tonton Jules. We give her carte blanche, money's no object. The only constraints are that it's to be a restaurant in this place, this street, this city. We're so comfortably funded that Claire could have the tables built of gold if she chose, and there's no deadline, she can take years if need be."

"Sure," says Jacquot. "Hirohito's summer palace and Mitsubishi's corporate headquarters will just have to go to the back burner. Claire's doing it partly for old times' sake, too, not just for the bucks."

"Of course not—dough's merely an enabling device. So workmen come and go for a year, carrying out old Claire's orders, all sworn to secrecy, until at last it's done. Claire meets us and the news crews at the door. This is her masterpiece, we can tell clear as anything just from her face."

"Her modesty," Jeremy says, "her exhilaration."

"Her peace," adds Jacquot.

"This is it, all right. The reporters trooping in behind us know, too. So what we find inside . . ." Jeremy and Jacquot glance at each other, enjoying the moment. Yannic inhales. "What we find is exactly what's beneath us now. Down to the finest detail, each peeling and smudge, the laughable wallpaper, the cigarette holes in the oilcloth. The calendar outdated by precisely that much, everything was deliberate. Any number of spiders had been tried, arachnologists consulted, before the sort that could be induced to make precisely that raggedy web near the ceiling had been found. It was far and away the most complete décor anyone had ever done, ever."

Jacquot smiles and nods. "And?"

Yannic with a questioning look gives Jeremy a chance to take up the story. Jeremy returns the floor to Yannic with an open hand. A curtain of dark shining rain blows against the windowpanes. Yannic sighs. "Clair's amply rewarded, in hard cash and in worldwide acclaim, and she wends her way back to the Land of the Rising Sun a little regretfully. She knows it'll be downhill after Tonton Jules."

"And his nephew," Jacquot can't resist adding.

"We record the place for posterity with videotapes and laser grams and air samples, but as opening night draws near we start to have second thoughts, until we're forced to admit that after all we really don't much want to work inside a national monument. Business would boom but it just wouldn't exactly be our business. We'd be inhibited. So upon reflection we decide to change the décor."

"Undo Claire's triumph?" Jacquot sounds proprietary.

Jeremy muses, "It would change anyway, of course."

Yannic says, "It would, but Claire had factored those changes in already. Silly us, we wanted an ambience, a look we could forget about because it was our own, with all its lapses and grossnesses. So we went to work ourselves, and altered it."

"We altered it," Jacquot breathes. Down in the cold wet street a car shushes and creaks. Twinkling rain vanishes on the windows of the empty room. The car door clicks and clunks, and high heels clop-clop across the cobbles.

Jeremy says, "The point is . . ."

"The point." Yannic tugs the crease of a cuff of his trousers. "One point is, we'll never create a décor *ex nihilo* any more than Claire did. Trying to do that would be like trying to create a color—it can't be done."

"Lots would differ with you there," Jacquot says. "Couturiers, advertisers for house paint. They're interested, of course."

Yannic nods. "The new thing they create is only a name for a color, a way of cordoning off a color and looking at it. What we'll be doing is even simpler, in a way. We'll just be changing a décor. From what it is to what it'll be when we're done."

Jeremy says, "I think he's on to something. Claire's secret, maybe: don't create, change. How though? I move we adopt some rules of thumb."

"Thumb?"

"Principles, like this: make it slow burn."

"Burn?"

"I mean it shouldn't be too much of a piece. Not a mermaid's grotto or a Dublin pub or whatever with everything chosen accordingly, not a theme park. It should all be of a piece, but not that way. The criteria shouldn't be so obvious."

"No?"

"No, because then it can all be . . . dismissed."

Jacquot twiddles a shred of ham over his paper plate. "I'm thinking we ought to use screens or something to break up the space—not that there's so much of it—and mirrors to complicate it a little more. The lighting should probably be soft. Candles on tables maybe. Soothing plants."

Jeremy sits up. "Sounds good to me, but what about our principles? Listen, I propose that we create—change—the décor in tandem. Each works a while on one part and then shifts and works on a part somebody else has been working on. Like that, till the whole thing has a natural homogeneity."

Yannic says, "Beautiful. Wouldn't it take forever though?"

Jacquot shakes his head. "It might accelerate in and of itself. Except, what's a part? A wall? A quadrant?"

"Maybe," says Jeremy.

"What about the music then?"

"That's a part too."

Jacquot turns to Yannic. "He's right—we don't need to catalogue in advance. Parts reveal themselves. I vote for Jeremy's plan."

"Me too, I guess," says Yannic. "Even though it does sound sort of utopian."

"I'll make it unanimous," says Jeremy. "Let's drink to it."

They drink to Jeremy's plan and to a great deal more as rain clears through this night. During the following weeks, catch as catch can the scheme works and the established décor, eclectic and dapper in a subdued way, obliging yet not quite ingratiating, controls from then on. When any further change is considered the question is, Does it fit with what's there, is it in keeping? Nine times out of ten the answer is immediately apparent.

3. *Politics*

Jacquot, the most unfailingly cheerful of the three young men, privately harbors the greatest reservations about their common enterprise, as is to be expected, because the premises remains his. If the enterprise succeeds it will be easy to share credit, but Jacquot suspects that the weight of any failure will fall more on him, for having drawn in his friends. And there's another reason for his tacit doubt. Not often, but sometimes, he's troubled by his colleagues' being lovers. It isn't so much that they're gay rather than straight, it's that they're lovers, each other's, neither his.

He remembers a time in Montréal when he and Claire had a common friend, Suzanne, who actually introduced them. He and Suzanne had spent some time together, made love once or twice, and had amicably concluded that further developments in that direction weren't in order. Therefore no question of jealousy or envy arose when he and Suzanne's friend of several years hit it off better. Really none, so far as Jacquot can see. The three of them had taken an apartment and for six weeks it had seemed to work but then things started to go wrong. They stuck it out for another couple of months and then finally Suzanne moved to a smaller apartment in the building and Jacquot and Claire to a smaller one in a different building. It was bad, maybe it was what had started Jacquot's hair graying prematurely.

Jacquot thinks it wouldn't have happened if he and Claire hadn't been lovers. Despite Suzanne's natural crotchetiness the three had been on good terms and it should have been easy to live together, but it wasn't. Now in retrospect Jacquot believes his major error was a solicitous readiness to ally himself with Suzanne or to have her and Claire allied against him in minor questions, like who was to wash the windows—an excessive avoidance of siding with Claire against Suzanne. It only made Suzanne believe what it had been meant to make her not believe: that in the privacy of their bedroom he and Claire were reaching decisions about washing the windows, that fucking made them a caucus. It wasn't really true but in a sense it became true, and worse did. They hadn't found a way to buck it. Now, with Jeremy and Yannic, Jacquot holds Suzanne's position. He wants the disquieting memory to help him recognize any first symptoms of such a turn of events and steer clear.

The trio avoids this and other potential sidetracks inherent in its asymmetry, as the restaurant proves itself a qualified success. Yannic and Jeremy keep the sometimes rocky course of their love to themselves, and Jacquot's close association does not make it any rockier. He is desirable to be sure, but early on both Jeremy and Yannic have decided not to desire him, in the kind of reflex decision desirable people prompt regularly.

The Tonton Jules Corporation with its three equal shareholders leases the building from Jacquot for the amount of taxes and upkeep. Yannic and Jeremy occupy the second floor, and Jacquot the garret. The utopian rotation of the decorating continues in work assignment, as the trio revolves through chef, sous-chef, waiter, and dishwasher. Each chef develops special dishes which may then be featured on his or another's evening. They pay a fair salary to themselves and a generous wage to the part-time cashiers, bussers, and waiters, including foxy Danielle Hébert from up the street who flirts with all three of them and now and again lands herself a visit to the garret.

Menus are in French only. As everyone says, the current flow of Québecois nationalism will probably peak and then ebb without altering the landscape, as has happened in the past. Still, separatism definitely is in the air at the moment, and authorities have given up trying to prevent vandals from painting out the English on bilingual signs in any but the best-policed streets of the upper town.

Among themselves the restaurateurs speak French almost exclusively. It is Jacquot's and Yannic's first language, though both have studied some English, and Yannic who grew up in B.C. has a fair proficiency. Jeremy knows he will never achieve perfect fluency in either Yannic's Norman-inflected French or Jacquot's Québecois laced with the argot of *joual*, but he has an ear and he progresses rapidly enough, and he is pleased to abandon what a U.S. poet is calling "the language of the oppressor." He believes that his linguistic migration also helps with early-morning work on a study begun as a dissertation at Chicago. While Yannic snores in the bedroom, Jeremy in his green eye shade subjects English sentences to successive transformations and asks of each result, "Is this still good English? Has the meaning changed?" and, when a number of sentences have undergone the same transformations, he examines each stage for minutest divergences from the parallel.

Jeremy has learned to do this kind of investigation from reading the celebrated linguist Noam Chomsky, whose influence has declined only slightly from its height during Jeremy's Chicago days, and partly because the man now writes not only about language but also about the U.S. expenditure of lives and parts of lives in Southeast Asia. Jeremy wonders whether Chomsky associates proving moral truth with proving linguistic truth. Jeremy does. He believes that life unlike ours uses languages in millions of places in the universe; and he believes that the grammar that would generate all his own species' languages must itself be generated by the deepest of all grammars, which underlies all and only languages in the universe, by virtue of which translation must be possible from any to any. Similarly he believes that the deep morality of his species, which all members know, though its formulations are piecemeal and halting, must be intelligible universally—so that, for instance, the inexcusability of the current U.S. vice-presidential nominee Rockefeller's having many millions of times the power that all but a few like him have must be intelligible not just generally on the planet, but quite generally. And Jeremy believes that the deepest generative morality must have much to do with the deepest grammar, if not be identical with it.

When Jeremy airs some of these beliefs with Yannic at breakfast late in the restaurant's first April, the subject of Yannic's inheritance arises. All his time with Jeremy, indeed all his adult life, he has lived more or less as if it didn't exist, the trust fund at his disposal and the far larger sum he will inherit from his father. But now, liking working to keep the restaurant going makes him feel ready to look straight at the fact of his family's wealth, and to come to terms with it and take action. He and Jeremy have moved the breakfast table halfway onto their narrow balcony, into the spring light. Pigeons clatter away from a bicycle in the street below. Yannic says, "If I were a magician, if I could snap my fingers and make it vanish, I think I'd have done it long ago. Would giving it away be the right thing to do?"

Jeremy thinks. "Are you sure you could? Wouldn't your family be able to subvert anything you tried—arrange for the money to be kept from you till you're older and wiser?"

"No, Jeremy, it really is possible to waive all claim. My Aunt Léonie did it with some money she was inheriting. It was a gesture of contempt for whoever had left it to her. She signed it over to a religious order. Later she decided she wanted it back because the group was adopting overtly progressive political positions. She sued, but she ended up losing."

"Okay, so giving it away works. Who to?"

"Does it matter?"

"ITT?"

Yannic smiles. "I just meant it'll be out of my hands, whoever takes it."

"I know. Listen, how about . . ." Jeremy's face goes blank and he tucks his hands under the waistband of his jeans, "how about giving it to me?"

Yannic laughs. "You want it? It's yours," he says, and then after a moment, "You want it?"

Jeremy shrugs and lifts his coffee bowl.

"Does this mean you have an idea? I haven't been your sugar daddy, but maybe you'd like being mine."

Jeremy says, "Maybe yours, maybe. You know, though, I was thinking about when I was growing up in Cleveland. People used to say we in the U.S. had a higher standard of living than people anywhere else. Well, it was naïve—bigger cars, color television, and the per-capita income was only a simple average, and doctored at that. But the point is that we—because of course I was a child of the only culture I knew—we didn't see anything wrong with being better off than everybody else. Quite the contrary: people boasted of it. Does your family boast of being richer than ninety-nine people in a hundred?"

"Ninety-nine point nine. Not out in front. When they boast it's about something like a painting they've bought—acquired, they say, found, picked up. They almost never mention how rich they are."

"Yannic?"

"Yeah."

"You can refuse their money but you can't prevent its being offered. And refusing the money won't alter your having been one of them. Nothing will. You can't erase your education, for instance, not short of lobotomy. But what you can do is put it to work, use it for better ends than it was designed for. Divert it. As you do. Why not the money too?"

"Okay, how—famine relief?" When Jeremy seems about to shrug again, Yannic continues, "Which famine then? And then what happens? The wad makes it past all the machinery designed to create famine, through levels upon levels of corrupt administration, diminishing all the way. It turns into food and diminishes in the distribution. Finally somewhere some people stop starving for a while. Then what, Jeremy?"

Jacquot on his way downstairs has stepped through his friends' doorway and come to the open balcony in time to hear Yannic's question. A breeze riffles corners of the morning paper kept in place with a dish of butter. After a moment Jeremy says, "All the same, I know everybody should eat. Eat well, have shelter, travel, be able to do anything anybody else does. The resources exist and anybody who says otherwise is a knave or a dupe. It can happen, and I assume it will."

"Hear, hear," says Jacquot.

4 *Wish Fulfillment*

Three young men, two Canadians and a Yank, join forces in the late seventies to establish Tonton Jules, a brave little restaurant in Québec's lower town that in its first month of operation draws not only curious residents of the neighborhood, adjoining neighborhoods, the upper town and even an outlying portion of greater Québec, but also visitors from as far away as Montréal, Vancouver, and Cleveland. Heretofore they have dreamed and planned with the luxurious vagueness of youth, but running a restaurant is harder work than they had imagined, especially in the beginning, and above all in the crucial second year—novelty value has waned, while Tonton Jules is still too young to be a gastronomic landmark without a giant advertising budget. Patrons seem pleased, they have no ptomaine or broken teeth, and Jeremy averts the only near-disaster with a Heimlich maneuver. Smokers and nonsmokers, carnivores and vegetarians can be accommodated. The restaurateurs keep informal tabs on repeat customers and those drawn by word of mouth, and congratulate themselves when they have cause. They celebrate an appreciative card in the afternoon mail with champagne. Still, a slow week leads them to hash over the seemingly insoluble parking problem yet again, and even to wonder whether the public, fickle as birds, can't simply have altogether left behind its interest in eating. A slow week leads them to work harder than ever to please, and there are enough slow weeks in the first and second years to give their lives a very tight focus.

Jacquot finds less and less time for piano, Jeremy less time for modal auxiliaries and less for the United States even though he has been granted amnesty by the second winter, Yannic less time for memories and dreams of further travel. In the second winter, with coffers bare and the carnival above drawing the most dependable repeaters to the upper town, who should slip in with a handsome woman on his arm but the restaurant critic of *Le Soleil*. The staff performs with hypnotic alertness. The critic seems interested in the *rillettes*, and perhaps in Yannic's father's cook's Norman *tarte*.

In the morning Jacquot, first down, steps out to open the blue shutters and scoop the paper off the snow. Inside at the front table he finds no verdict on Tonton Jules in the rattling paper but a review does catch his eye, of a recital that took place last weekend at Laval University, the performer a pianist he studied with back in Montréal.

It's a bit of a jolt. A year and a half, two years ago he'd have attended the concert, known about it weeks in advance, and known what to make of the generally unfavorable review too. The playing described bears little resemblance to what Jacquot remembers of the pianist's strengths and weakness, but he knows no one to ask about it, he realizes. On three paper coasters from the sideboard he writes the pianist herself a note of bewilderment. She replies soon and graciously, recounting changes in her playing and mentioning some of the reviewer's idiosyncracies in such a way as to reduce the mystery. The letter makes Jacquot high.

It also makes Jacquot low. He wishes he'd heard the recital, to hear and think over and talk more about those changes in her playing, and he realizes he misses playing enough for analogous changes of his own to come about. He arranges to use a practice room at Laval three mornings a week for three hours starting in January. It goes well again, as well as before the restaurant. Once he's worked out the initial stiffness he reaches a plateau, but still it's good, and not just as investment for a time when he might have more time. Maybe it's all to the good, because playing on that plateau becomes a way of thinking about music, and the difference between the playing and the music diminishes toward zero and often the music plays him as much as the reverse.

Claire writes from a Hokkaido ski lodge. Tokyo interiors aren't exactly crying out for Western decorators, and she has smelled unpleasantly milky to two men in a row, but she plans to stay on. She misses Jacquot and hopes he'll keep in touch and visit when the exchange rate permits. Jacquot thinks he can find a ghost of Claire's old perfume on the rice paper.

In February Jacquot takes the practice room for a fourth morning. It's too late for him to make a career of performing—at least any kind of career he'd want, at least it seems so—and as he plays on through the snowy winter and cold spring he sees that there are kinds and depths of understanding music he's scarcely dreamed of, and others and others after those, surely without end. Nevertheless, undeterred, Jacquot keeps on keeping on through the spring and summer, and by September he's ready to put together a trio, and before the first snowfall they open for a month of weekends back in Montréal. Yannic and Jeremy attend, and so do family and friends, and so does Danielle Hébert from the restaurant. Jacquot dedicates a fusion stride Vigneault, "Ma Jeunesse," to her. Good reviews for the trio and (at last) for Tonton Jules lead Jacquot to cut his partnership in the restaurant in half so as to give his music more room, and the arrangement seems to work. In April he and Danielle marry. She continues half-time at the restaurant—there will be time for children later. Danielle loves her musical fox, and she continues to flirt with Jeremy and with Yannic when she sees him.

5. *Souvenirs*

In all directions the white flat-roofed houses have closed blue shutters against the glare. Disturbed palm leaves rustle above a garden wall. Yannic Demombynes slips off his backpack and lets it slide down to the hot streetbed. Something has gone wrong. Ahead, the street rises to a bridge over the river that separates the new village from the old, where Hammed's family supposedly lives. A camel's head, a whole camel sways over the bridge and disappears between houses to the left. Someone has misunderstood a message. At the shed back in the square Yannic has waited past the arrival of the nine o'clock bus from Tunis, and past the next at eleven. No Hammed though. But does it matter?—that an heir of a Vancouver lumber fortune, orphaned in his midthirties and now pushing forty, should miss a meeting with a twenty-year-old Tunisian on leave from army duty on the island where they met a month ago, and arranged to meet again here? Maybe Hammed has been waiting at the bus stop an hour away in Tunis, and has given up, and is on his way here. Whatever, Yannic thinks he will locate Hammed's father's house and pay respects.

These six months of overdue vagabondage in North Africa have seemed almost a return to the months in Colombia, back before the cocaine trade severed communications with all friends there, and Yannic knows the welcome to expect at Hammed's parent's house, the greatly desirable welcome of poor people who know next to nothing of him. Why so desirable? Hammed himself might be willing to accommodate any desires his purplish eyes should have prompted, but Yannic hasn't made his way to this outlying village for that. Even before the AIDS panic the story would have been much the same—Yannic's need for people like Hammed is sexual only at a great remove.

It's still suspect though, Yannic now thinks, with a hot dry breeze cooling his neck. It's suspect exactly in the key of heterosexuality, this abiding need for the poor, this desire for what he neither is nor ever will be. Jeremy will mock him for it again surely, in a letter or in their bed. Jeremy will again call him romantic or sentimental, some kind of dupe. Those accusations have lost all force, though, and Yannic's wealth no longer troubles him much. Life is too short. For that matter, Yannic now thinks, looking over the blue and white village into the white sky, isn't the wish for justice itself a kind of sentimentality? Yannic picks up the pack and works his arms into the harness. Hammed's names seem too common to identify him even in a village this small, but still with his age and his army status it might be possible to find the way to his house.

Jeremy Stein raises the garret window and looks out. Down at the corner workmen are clearing away the foundations of the condemned house now giving way to restaurant parking, "Parking," the sign will say, at once in English and in Anglicized French. Up the street a neighbor's child jumps rope in the brisk wind. Jeremy thinks he sees snow in the graying sky.

He has been moving books and documents, the restaurant's and his own, into the garret that has stood empty since Jacquot and Danielle moved to the suburbs. He has been thumbing through old letters from Cleveland, letters from Yannic, and pages of his unfinished dissertation, and he has been thinking about erasure. Blanket amnesty has long since erased the "guilt" of his war resistance, and he has been able to return to Cleveland for his father's funeral and again later for his mother's remarriage. But of course the barrier between him and his native nation has stood on, "under erasure," in the phrase the philosopher Jacques Derrida has given currency. So, Jeremy thinks, contradictions south of the border have persisted under the erasure of the first Reagen term and half of the second, until the recent thinning of that erasure.

Jeremy has been thinking about the erasure of ideals and of hope that the current intellectual climate seems to foster, and that age—middle age anyway—certainly is fostering in him. "All the same," he says. All the same, Québec will live under the snow that partly erases it.

Out a window two floors above the restaurant, most of whose management has devolved upon him, Jeremy Stein looks at the people in the street, the workmen, the child at play, and now a grandmother setting out for the morning's shopping.

At a luggage carousel at Dorval in Montréal, a late Tuesday in a weathery April, Jacquot Loubet shifts his sleeping infant daughter, Oriane, in her carrier slung across his back. "We tried to keep her up for you, Yannic. In a couple of hours she'll be wide awake again, but you probably want a rain check for the two o'clock feeding. What time is it for you, anyway?"

As ashen Yannic struggles to make the computation, Jeremy answers for him, "The middle of next week." He rumples Yannic's curls. "A few more silver threads among the gold there."

"Distinguished," offers Jacquot, himself prematurely silvered. "Come through Paris?"

"Cairo, Paris, Montréal. Security tight as a drum. I've never been patted down before."

Jacquot's eyes twinkle. "Not in an airport anyway. Well, he's looking good, isn't he, Jeremy. How's about us?"

One by one the pieces of luggage nose forward through the flapping rubber. Weary Canadians and foreigners Yannic has crossed the North Atlantic with summon one last surge of alertness, as with families and friends they survey the motley file advancing. Yannic says, "Even asleep, Oriane looks like a future prime minister."

"Asleep mainly, maybe."

Yannic nods. "And fatherhood seems to be agreeing with you."

"And Jeremy?" Jacquot holds Jeremy's shoulders like a coach displaying an athlete. "Have we taken good care of this one for you, or what?"

Yannic lays a hand over Jeremy's middle. "Maybe too good. You've let his hairline recede some more though."

Jeremy shakes his head. "No matter, they've found a cure for baldness. Where've you been, boy? Time we got you back into civilization."

Jacquot nods. "Back into the business world. We have big plans for the restaurant."

"Jacquot does anyway."

Yannic smiles. People and luggage jostle around him. His fellow travelers have recovered from the abstracted silence that deepened through the flight, and irrelevant announcements of new arrivals and departures sink in the din. Yannic kneads his neck and watches the rubber flaps. "Here comes at least one of mine. We'll keep our fingers crossed."

Hillcrest Days

Marie Tester has killed two people, one quite by accident. Thirty-odd years ago, back when she was still in North Dakota where there were no mountains and no ocean (Marie liked it wide open where you could see forever unless it was snowing), she had her snow chains on so she couldn't have been going at all fast even if she was late to work. It was a stranger who practically jumped into her headlights and another stranger in the stalled Alberta car saw it happen. That was more than thirty years ago, before dawn in January. She worked in a café forty miles away glad of the job, nine, ten hours six days for what would be nothing now. She'd have been near twenty. The stranger was dead by the time she got out of the car and the other one testified to her innocence. The café let her off for the deposition.

The other person Marie killed was her sister, let's say. It was far slower and more recent. It wasn't murder either. It wasn't manslaughter either. Marie Tester killed her sister with unkindness and her sister was dying anyway. Her older sister who'd followed her to Seattle.

The year is 1976. Marie Tester is a bit overweight the way lots of people her age are, and short. When she talks to you and you're a couple of heads taller she mostly looks at whatever she has in her hands or at her empty hands, at her bad nails and then whenever she does look at your face she doesn't tilt hers up, she just raises her eyes and it's like the glance of a dog lying on the floor. She's drinking more than she should these days. Well that's nothing new. More than she used to then and not just in the Sportsman's Lounge (used to be the Tip Top) up the street, but also in her apartment alone with Trixie, her blonde cocker. Trixie's old and overweight too. She doesn't get anything like enough exercise. Pretty soon Marie's going to have Trixie put to sleep and then not get any other animals. You get attached to them and it's not worth it.

Was Seattle the name of a car in the forties? Because it was like one to the Marie of then who'd never been outside North Dakota and still hasn't been east of there or south or north, only west to Seattle. She lives on Capitol Hill in the Hillcrest Apartments. She's been resident manager there going on eight years, with her husband till last year when she threw him out, now alone. The neighborhood was better once. The Hillcrest had different kinds of people in it. Now, well look: Rachel, two couples of gay boys, a forty-year-old woman cabdriver and her mother, the pair of old Lithuanian women in the basement terrified of everything—they pay $60 a month for the two unconnected rooms and a bath they share, they know Marie has no say about the rent and still they lay the politeness on like butter as if that way they could keep the rent from going up. They don't know what they'd do if it went up again. It will, they'll eat less, who knows.

Rachel Padilla is twenty-two, Chicana, pretty, independent with a mind of her own. Since all the apartments in the Hillcrest are furnished (except Marie's—she has her own furnishings), pets and children aren't allowed. Yet Rachel has a cat, Joshua. When Marie found out about Joshua and confronted Rachel, Rachel claimed not to have known it was against the rules. "Who made that rule anyway, you? Why don't you change it. Joshua's outside most of the time and when he has to do his business he asks me to let him out. Josh and I are friends, I can't send him down the river."

Marie sputtered in the doorway. "Listen, Rachel. I'm the manager here. I've been managing this building twelve years and you've only been here what is it, two months? You're like a guest in my house here. You'll just have to obey the rules, I mean it Rachel! You signed the rental agreement, it's too bad if you didn't read it, you were supposed to. It says no animals. Take a look at it, you have a copy. I gave you one."

Rachel gave Marie a troublemaker's cool appraising look. "I'll think it over. I guess the owner's name's on my copy of that agreement. Maybe I should get in touch with him. You're not a bad manager but there's probably a lot he doesn't know about. I'll think it over and let you know."

Then for a week Marie was in a dither. At the Group Health Emergency Room—it wasn't just a room, more of a little hospital six blocks from the Hillcrest, Marie worked three nights as a cleaning lady—mopping the corridors she'd bend the other cleaning ladies' ears about Rachel. Afternoons when she and Trixie were out for a walk around the neighborhood she'd be mulling it over, Trixie got more than one earful about Rachel that week and so did Marie's fellow regulars at the Sportsman's. So did a number of Hillcrest tenants, though Marie began more circumspectly with them. From her second-floor window she'd see one of them step out of the bus at the corner. She'd light a cigarette and go out into the hallway with an ashtray in her hand, up to the third floor, back along the hallway, timing it. She'd listen for footsteps and then start back, pass the tenant with a preoccupied air ("Oh, hi there Alan") and then turn. "Alan can I speak with you. Has Rachel been saying anything to you boys about me? She's a troublemaker and I think I'm going to have to give her an eviction notice."

The owner of the Hillcrest lives in a suburb on the other

side of Lake Washington. He's a retired doctor, a widower with two married children who live far away. He owns another apartment building on Capitol Hill and another in West Seattle. They're much alike. He acquired them all in the late fifties. Marie mails him the rent a little after the first of the month. He came to this country as a boy, from eastern Europe.

He stops by the Hillcrest to look at the damage a spiteful tenant has done one of the apartments. The tenant had a pot of marijuana in his window. Marie wasn't sure but she thought it was, so she asked him, he said yes, she told him to dispose of it. "It's against the law, isn't it?" she asked another of the younger tenants. The marijuana grower moved out in the middle of the night (while Marie was at the Emergency Room) with half a month's rent owing. For spite he'd poured a gallon of molasses onto the carpet and dumped the dirt from his marijuana pot into it. Marie wanted the owner to see the mess before she rented a rug shampooer. He wanted to look over the building for two reasons he didn't mention to Marie. Because an old woman had died in an apartment-house fire, the city was starting to enforce fire laws more, and the Hillcrest would probably have to have fire walls and doors built in the corridors. Also the owner was planning to sell the building and he wanted to have a look at some of the apartments to remind himself what they were like. Marie introduced him to one of the gay couples, who'd moved in two weeks before. He glanced around. So did Marie. The gay couple didn't seem to have many belongings. They'd rearranged the furniture and taped odd but not dirty pictures on the walls. "By the way, Ms. Tester, when you get a chance could you give us a copy of the rental agreement? Whenever." "Yes, yes," Marie muttered. She was supposed to have given them a copy when they moved in but her typewriter was on the blink. The rental agreement forbade attaching pictures or anything else to the walls. The owner noticed but didn't mention it.

When Marie threw her husband out she threw out everything in the apartment too. Tableware, couch, drapes, rug—she might have sold some of it or the Salvation Army would have been glad of it but Marie threw it in the garbage, left it out for the trash collector. "I'm Irish and I have a temper," she warns you. Both her parents were born in North Dakota and so was she, but one of her grandparents was from Ireland and two others had ancestors there.

Rachel sleeps with her jewelry and makeup on. She likes to wear clothes from the forties, from before she was born. She finds them in thrift stores, especially the Goodwill down in the city market. This year at the market fair bands played from a rooftop all day Saturday. The weather was hot and perfect. The market complex and the narrow streets were packed with different people having a good time, all different sorts of people, different ages, talking to strangers, sharing food and drink and dope perfectly naturally. Rachel was there. In the afternoon she was dancing in one place with different individuals for more than two hours except for the ten minutes it took her to change from one forties dress (whose seam was splitting) into another. She was stoned and dancing well, sweating like a horse. She was wearing the jewelry she wears when she sleeps—she doesn't even take it off in the shower. One of the bands released fifty red balloons into the blue sky as it played.

When Marie threw her husband out she meant it to be permanent. Divorce seemed right but she had no idea how to go about it or what the laws were. Someone suggested the legal-aid society. Its office was down the hill in a mainly black section on a busy street. It turned out to be simpler than she'd expected, and cheaper, so she went through with it. Since then her husband's shown up once or twice at the Hillcrest, always drunk. One afternoon he came banging on the door of her apartment. Marie attached the chain lock and opened the door a crack. Goddamn it let me in, you're my wife, I want in.

Marie's dander was up. I'm not your goddamn wife anymore and if you don't stop that racket and get the hell out of this building I'll call the police!

Not that they'd come nowadays. Last summer the crowd of young people in the house next-door were having some kind of party carousing and playing loud music in the middle of the day when Marie had to sleep. She threw up her window and yelled at them to can the racket or else. They laughed. The police receptionist said she'd pass the complaint on but the party was still going strong when Marie left for work at ten that night.

When somebody threw a brick through the building's glass front door in the middle of the winter Marie wondered if it was one of them, or the tenant who'd poured molasses on the rug, or her husband. It happened at night and it was cold. One of the tenants taped dry cleaner's thin plastic over the hole but still the temperature was way down when Marie got back from work and found it. Mrs. Kundrata, one of the Lithuanian women, told Rachel darkly she thought she knew who did it but couldn't say.

The mention of police didn't faze Marie's husband, he was so drunk. Finally she undid the chain lock and let him in. He put his fists to his head and glared. "What've you done?"

"Threw it all out!"

"Oh yeah?" He got a shifty look on his face.

"What the hell do you want anyway?"

He slumped down on the new used sofa.

"What the hell do you want!"

"Come on, Marie."

"Now, now you don't have any business here now!" She got him out after an hour that time. They'd both been yelling mad. He said he wanted to move back in because he'd been kicked out of his rooming house. That was a lie and anyway it was too damn late for that. Marie didn't think he'd hit her now they were divorced and if he'd tried to she could probably have dodged, he was drunk enough. Half the Hillcrest must've heard it though. The woman across the hall—been there going on two years, works nights at Boeing—it woke her up but she didn't complain, in fact she came over and invited Marie back to her place for a double shot of applejack. "It's not right, Marie," she said. "You shouldn't have to put up with that kind of behavior." Marie said, "You're damn right it's not right. I'll tell you this though: even if it was right it wouldn't do me any damn good!"

He stayed away a couple of months. He did get kicked out of his rooming house, and lost his job for drinking. He was in real trouble. Marie let him come back and sleep on her sofa for a week till he'd found work again and moved to another rooming house.

Rachel was visiting one of the gay couples and they had a wine bottle on a plate with a candle on it, the bottle covered with wax from earlier candles that had run down the bottle onto the plate. Rachel said, "I like your candle. You know what I was thinking though? I was thinking I'd like to have one and let it run out on the table and down onto the floor."

Marie leafed through a house-beautiful magazine under the dryer at La Nae Salon up the street. It had an article about weekend vacations in different cities for married couples who'd left their kids home, and one of the four cities happened to be Seattle. The article told what the couple would do Friday evening, Saturday daytime and evening, Sunday daytime. Marie read about Seattle's fascinating blend of diversions—a dinner theater that was a great place to forget little problems, pubs worth poking into, the Space Needle, colorful survivors from another era in Olde Seattle, unique eateries, atmosphere, marine-oriented attractions, several interesting shops if a bit more browsing seems in order, Pioneer Banque, top jazz performers. . . . Marie wondered if there were people it would sound real to, who'd read it and come to Seattle and have a weekend like the one in the article. The article priced the weekend at $184, broken down into categories. But who in their right mind would pay $40 a night for a hotel room? It seemed like a joke or an insult. Marie looked at the cover of the magazine. It showed a pie and two cakes. She flipped back to the article.

When Marie left North Dakota and came to Seattle of her own accord nobody was holding a gun to her head. She chose to be resident manager of the Hillcrest of her own free will. The soles of her feet are wrinkled white with pumpkin-yellow thick callouses—ugly and pathetic, but whose fault is that? Marie could have bettered herself but she didn't. Other people become brain surgeons, stars, chairmen of boards of blue-chip corporations, buy goods and services advertised in magazines Marie's never opened in her life. They become ambassadors and presidents and have incomes in the upper six figures. Nobody with a gun said, "Marie, choose a life with few choices or else." The *Who's Who* editor didn't send her mother a telegram, "New daughter eliminated. Regrets." Apparently Marie didn't care to be listed in that book. In a sense she even chose her carroty callouses, her basset gaze.

The week after she let her husband sleep on her sofa, when on top of everything else she found $50 missing—money she needed especially then, as will be seen—when she took the tea pot out from behind other dishes and found it empty she knew her husband had stolen the money and the first feeling she had was an angry sadness for him that he'd had to stoop so low and that even though he'd never admit it to her or probably anybody the knowledge would add a little to his shame and before he died he'd come to stoop some lower because of it. What Marie felt first off standing there in her kitchen was angrily sorry for him, and no law said she had to find herself in such a pickle.

Let's say the other person Marie killed wasn't her sister. Let's say it was you. Let's say the eyes are dead, moving back and forth, back and forth, moving but dead. How did she do it. Why. Was it quite accidental. Are there extenuating circumstances. Let's say one of the furnishings Marie threw out when she threw out her husband was a metronome. It had never been any use—Marie's not musical, her husband either—it was just there doing her no good in the world. Let's try that one on for size.

Rachel's mother lives in Tacoma. In Texas when Rachel was growing up she and her mother didn't get along too good. There were certain things her mother didn't want her to do—like having sex with certain individuals—and when she found out she'd beat Rachel. When Rachel got busted for dope her mother had her sent to a reform school. But now Rachel and her mother get along fine, have a good time together. Rachel's father's dead. He was a Mexican without papers to be in this country, a wetback. Rachel thinks he was into dealing drugs of some kind. He'd be away for long times at a time, then show up with money and tequila. Rachel loved him. He'd been gone a long time and Rachel asked her mother when he was coming back—it was the first time she'd ever asked that—and her mother said he was dead, she'd been meaning to tell Rachel. A year or so later Rachel found out he'd committed suicide. It was in a vision she had. He'd got caught with drugs and he was an illegal alien, he was in a dirty little jail and he knew they'd keep him in jail for maybe the rest of his life so he hanged himself, Rachel saw him do it. Marie's parents have both been gone for decades.

Early one morning Marie was having trouble sleeping so she'd got up and was reading the paper in the living room. She heard a whack! sudden brakes and a yelping. It was the dog from the house next door, those damn irresponsible kids. Marie threw up her window. The dog's owner'd come out of the house, the driver was out of the car explaining how it happened, the dog had run right out in front of the car. The dog was yelping almost without a voice, trying to get on its feet. Marie yelled at the boy. "It's your own damn fault. You let it run loose and don't teach it to stay out of the street. It was bound to happen sooner or later."

If you have a dog you have to take care of it. Any animal. Rachel's cat Joshua. You have to feed it and take care of it, and you have to teach it things. To stay out of the street. Because they don't know, they think cars'll stop for them. You have to teach them, otherwise you shouldn't have them, you might as well put them to sleep right off the bat.

Rachel's Joshua started losing weight and hair this February. Rachel didn't know at first. Insofar as possible she wanted him to have the same rights and privileges as she so she let him go out when he wanted and sometimes he stayed away four, five days. "Who ya been ballin', Josh?" she said when he dragged himself back sick. After a week he was worse and Rachel took him to a vet down on Twelfth Street. The vet said Josh would die unless he had a $45 operation and even then he'd only have a 30 percent chance. The vet said he'd put him to sleep if he was his. It took Rachel a couple of days to decide. For herself she might have tried herbal medicine but she was in the dark about cat herbs. Marie said, "He's a nice cat, Rachel, I like Joshua. I don't know though if I'd spend the money. Trixie'll have to be put to sleep before long. How're your plants doing?" Finally Josh had the operation. He was sick as a dog for a while but he's pulled through, gained his weight back and grown a new coat, and his aura's good as ever.

Marie's sister followed her to Seattle and lived with Marie and Marie's husband at first, then by herself, then with her own husband in Tacoma. The four of them got together sometimes. Marie's sister's husband's been dead almost twenty years now. Ten years back Marie's sister started to get sick. Six goddamn years in a hospital in Tacoma. We all have to die.

This winter there was only one real snow in Seattle, it was two days before Christmas. We had a white Christmas. One of the gay couples—the one in the apartment above Marie's—had a woman staying with them. She was the cousin-in-law of one of them, she'd come all the way from Washington, D.C., on a bus. She was French and she'd only been in this country two years. She probably didn't have anybody else to eat Christmas dinner with. She wore shoes with wooden soles. She had a nice face but the shoes were terrible on the stairs and over Marie's head. Marie stood it for a day and then when she heard the wooden shoes coming down the stairs past her doorway she threw open the door and said, "Listen, I can't have you running up and down in those loud shoes. This is supposed to be a quiet building—there are day sleepers here and anyway it's supposed to be quiet: that's why I don't allow children. Tenants aren't even supposed to have overnight guests but I can overlook that if it doesn't happen too often, but I can't have this noise. And another thing: when you're in your apartment tenants normally wear slippers. This building's old and the walls and floors and ceilings aren't at all soundproof." The woman said, "Yes?" and nodded like maybe she didn't understand, but one of her hosts was with her and he said, "Sorry." That wasn't the end of the story though.

The French woman and her hosts and some of their friends had their dinner and opened presents on Christmas Eve in the hosts' apartment. They put in the turkey around three. Someone had brought over a record player. It hadn't been on long before they heard Marie clinking on the water pipes. They turned down the volume. After fifteen minutes they heard the clink-clink again. It angered them some, but still they turned the volume down more. The dinner went well, they drank a lot of wine, talked and laughed. Around ten they found a note shoved under their door. It said, "I can't sleep because of your loud party. Very inconsiderate." The French woman's cousin-in-law—he was French too—said, "It's anonymous. Why couldn't the person who wrote it just come to the door and tell us?" They tried to be quieter. It was after midnight and they were in the middle of opening presents, many of which were comical, when Marie rapped on the door. "The rental agreement says no guests after 10:00 p.m. and no loud parties. I've had three complaints since I got off work and I'm sure to have more tomorrow. Now this is just intolerable." The French woman's cousin-in-law said, "It's Christmas Eve! We haven't made any noise for three months." Marie shook her head. "People here don't give one goddamn about Christmas Eve. They have to work and they have to sleep whatever damn day it is."

Marie's sick sister started talking garbage about faith and theosophy curing her bones four years back when she first had to stay in the hospital. Marie hated going to visit Saturdays or Sundays. Her damn husband hadn't once gone with her either. It was four buses and two cabs—Seattle number twelve down to the station, Greyhound to Tacoma, cab to the hospital and vice versa but it wasn't that so much, it was more the hospital itself. The building reminded you of the Hillcrest, down-at-heels brick from the same era. And the floors! If Marie let a floor go like that in the Emergency Room she'd get walking papers before the next shift. But mostly it was Marie's sister herself. Her gray broom spread out on the pillow. The weight she'd lost, her bad color. If she was conscious, her mind wandered. It was thirty years ago, they were rich not poor, staying at some kind of lodge in Bismark, Marie was their mother. "Mmm-hmm, mmm-hmm," Marie muttered. Except sometimes she got the feeling her sister knew it wasn't true, it was just a game she had to play and wanted Marie to play along with. When she wasn't wandering it was garbage about theosophy faith, whatever, always cheery as you please (the dope she was on), never chiding Marie for the visits she missed more and more. When she died Marie hadn't seen her in over two years. Marie's shift at the Emergency Room had just started when the call came. Marie knew she must've had terrible bedsores.

Wherever you live your gaze has slipped across the Hillcrest. From a car window in an unlikely neighborhood on your way somewhere else. Of course you've never set foot inside. Or if you have it wasn't to visit a friend or learn anything, unless by a fluke once, you didn't live there certainly or if you did it wasn't for long, not more than a year and it was years and years ago when you were alive, too long to remember. The Lithuanian women in the basement don't read about themselves, the people Marie reads about pay $40 a night for a hotel room. She looks at the cover. Two cakes and a pie. She tosses the magazine aside. Are there nonextenuating circumstances. Back and forth, back and forth.

Rachel dresses up to watch TV in one of her thrift-shop outfits including a fur stole and a hat she calls her Mouseketeer hat because of its exaggerated black felt bow. She turns her oven on to medium and leaves it open—it's a cold afternoon. The doorbell rings. Sometimes she doesn't answer. She turns the radio in her bedroom on loud enough to hear some of it back in the living room where the TV is. It's a very weird talk show on the TV. Rachel smokes some dope and watches. There's a knock at the door. It's one of the gay guys come to say hello. Rachel offers him some of the dope and some of the chili con carne she's made. They look at her plants and talk. Out her windows the light changes impressively through this late winter afternoon. Once a friend coming to visit Rachel saw her through the window in her stole and Mouseketeer hat and assumed she must be about to go out.

There aren't any roaches or ants in the Hillcrest, haven't been since Marie and her husband started being managers. She keeps the grass against the building cut and makes sure the foundation gets painted regularly with repellent. All the same it's good to have an aerosol can of insecticide handy. Marie kept hers in the cabinet under her bathroom sink.

One night this winter Marie came back from the Emergency Room and saw a fire truck and two police cars stopped at the Hillcrest with their blue lights on and turning, and a small crowd gathered. It was the week she let her husband sleep on her sofa. The aerosol insecticide can had exploded under Marie's bathroom sink, blown the sink off the wall. People in several apartments thought somebody'd knocked over a bookcase or something. Marie's husband on the sofa was too drunk for it to register. He didn't even wake up when the police and firemen broke open the door. The people in the apartment under Marie's had called them after they'd rung Marie's doorbell, knocked at her door and tried to telephone her (they were new and didn't know she'd be at work) about the water running through their ceiling. The commotion brought most of the tenants out into the stairwell. Marie's husband was on his feet but he still didn't understand what had happened. "Is there water in your place?" he asked one of the gay boys. "No—we live upstairs and water doesn't run uphill." "I know it doesn't," growled Marie's husband. Trixie was terrified. Rachel leaned over the banister. She had cherry-red toenails and she was wearing a matching silk nightgown and peignoir. "What's going on?" Marie's living-room rug she'd just finished paying for was ruined and she had no insurance. One of the gay boys advised her to write the insecticide company. "And who knows, there might be other dangerous cans of it in the area." Marie said, "And think if I'd been getting something out of that cabinet when it happened!"

Rachel got off the number-ten bus at the corner. It was one of those beautiful mild Capitol Hill June six o'clocks. Rachel didn't go in right away. She walked a couple of blocks to an intersection where you can see Mount Rainier if it's visible. That evening it was visible, a flamingo mountain floating in the sky in the southeast, it was beautiful. Rachel leaned against a street-sign pole, her ankles crossed, a posture she'd seen more than one woman assume in a forties movie on television. And in forties pictures, ads for cigarettes or whatever, women leaning against a pine tree or a lamppost, gazing at the moon with their ankles crossed just so, platform shoes, some kind of sophistication that was innocent and Rachel loved it. She stood there and smoked a cigarette watching Mount Rainier change from second to second. Nobody bothered her.

When she came back to the Hillcrest and was going in she met Marie. Marie said, "Oh, hi," as if she didn't remember who Rachel was. She was headed up the street to the convenience store whose red and green neon lighted the parking lot. Rachel went with Marie and they talked, Rachel knew something was wrong. "I was at the Emergency Room and they called up out of the blue just like that and told me my sister had died. I don't go to church or pray or anything, but this last year I've been wishing she would die if she wasn't going to get any better. She's been in the hospital six years. They didn't warn me though."

At the cash register Marie explained she was buying soap and toothpaste for her sister's niece who'd been called from Portland and had been with her when she died and now would be staying with Marie till the funeral. On an impulse Rachel said, "Here, let me buy it for you." Marie said no but Rachel insisted and the cashier told Marie, "Listen, it don't happen every day of the year, lady."

Marie doesn't go to church or pray or anything like that but this last year she's wished her sister would die if she wasn't going to get well. Marie never remembers her dreams and she hasn't driven since thirty-odd years ago in snowy North Dakota.

This June the gay couple over Marie moved out after a year there. They cleaned the apartment room by room, throwing away some things, giving away others, moving the rest into a corner of the living room and packing it into cartons to go east by train. They gave Rachel most of their plants and some thrift-shop dishes so as to have as little as possible in the car. They'd told Marie when they were leaving but sometimes pulling up stakes takes longer than you'd think and they were eight or nine days late getting off. Marie inspected the apartment the night before they left. "This is the part I hate. Now you owe me $42 rent for these extra days. I see you've done some work on the oven but I'll have to do it over, it's got to be completely clean. And I'll have to shampoo the rug too. Otherwise you've done a good job. Now the cleaning deposit was $50. What do you say if I take the rent you owe me out of it and keep the rest for the cleaning? You've been good tenants, always paid your rent on time. I'll miss you. I don't know how much longer I'll be here myself. The building's been sold. I've met the new owner and he and I didn't hit it off so good. I think I'll have to look for another building to manage." Workmen dismantled the big For Sale sign in the morning. The Lithuanian women watched out one of their basement windows.

Joe Ashby Porter is the author of *Eelgrass* and *The Kentucky Stories*, the latter a Pulitzer Prize nominee available from Johns Hopkins. Porter is associate professor of English at Duke University and has served as visiting fiction writer at Brown University. His works on Renaissance literature, published under the name Joseph A. Porter, include *Shakespeare's Mercutio: His History and Drama*.

Library of Congress Cataloging-in-Publication Data

Porter, Joseph Ashby, 1942–
Lithuania: short stories / by Joe Ashby Porter.
p. cm. — (Johns Hopkins, poetry and fiction)
ISBN 0-8018-4091-0 (alk. paper)
ISBN 0-8018-4092-9 (pbk.: alk. paper)
I. Title. II. Series.
PS3566.06515L58 1990
813′.54—dc20 90–36765 CIP

Stories in this collection appeared in slightly different form in the following anthologies and periodicals, to which the author and the publisher extend their thanks: "Aerial View" in *Louisville Review*; "Roof Work" in *Mid-American Review*; "Basse Ville" in *St. Andrews Review*; "Saint Silvère's Head" in *Archive* and *Confrontation*; "Attention, Shoppers" in *Witness*; "For Nineteen Sixty-eight" in *Iowa Review*; "Duckwalking" in *Contemporary American Fiction*, *Harper's*, and *Pushcart Prize IX: Best of the Small Presses*; "West Baltimore" in *American Voice*; "Retrieval" in *Raritan*; "Playing for Keeps" in *New American Writing*; and "Hillcrest Days" in *Cardinal* and *Via*.

LITHUANIA

Designed by Ann Walston

Composed by BookMasters, Inc.,
in Weiss with Weiss Italic display

Printed by The Maple Press Company
on 55-lb. Sebago Antique Cream